Little Stories for Grown Children

After Ever

D. Avery

After Ever by D. Avery

ISBN-10: 0692175474

ISBN-13: 978-0692175477

Exeter Press

Previously published stories include:
He Says and **Feedings** at *thedrabble.wordpress*; **The Cardigan** at
flashfictionmagazine.com; and **Licked** at *carrotranch.com* for the 2017 Flash
Fiction Rodeo's 9 x 11 Twitter Flash Contest.

To all who have endured me, entertained me, educated me, and encouraged me.

INTRODUCTION

Big stories can come in small packages. The majority of the short stories in this collection are flash fiction, written in response to on-line writing prompts with specific requirements, such as Charli Mill's *Carrot Ranch Flash Fiction Challenge* (99 words, no more, no less), or exactly six sentences for *Uncharted's* and then *Girlie On the Edge's* one word *Six Sentence Story* prompt; some were twitter flash challenges where the word count was less than fifty. While some of the flash responses presented here remain as they were for on-line publication, in many instances I did alter the word or sentence count through revising for this print publication.

The prompts often led to unexpected places and circumstances, dark and light. The prompts also brought forth enduring characters. Flash fiction often leaves room for interpretation and speculation, causing readers to wonder and want more; sometimes characters demanded more as well, and returned in succeeding prompts to have their stories continued. Flash fiction pieces that are linked by a recurring character or narrative are placed together in the book though separately on their own page, with the exception of *The Quill's Magic*.

I hope you enjoy reading these little stories.

THE QUILL'S MAGIC
THE GIFT

Once upon a time there was a king who had everything necessary and much that was imaginable and who always wanted more. He had a great many servants, among them a girl who tended to the horses in the royal stable.

One day the girl was surprised to find that the king's men had captured a large bird, which was kept in a locked stall. It fell to her to look after this strange creature.

She observed that every day this bird pulled one of its own feathers to make a writing quill, every day drew its own blood to use as ink that every day it might write its own story.

"Oh Bird, doesn't that hurt?"

"Yes, it hurts."

"Then why?"

"Because," the bird sighed, "at this time, in this place, I have no song."

The girl could not get the bird to eat or drink, could not get it to stop pulling its own feathers and drawing its own blood. She could not get it to stop writing. Unable to bear the pain of its silence, she stole the king's key and unlocked the stall door.

"Go," she urged, "while you still have feathers enough to escape."

The bird thanked her and took flight and as it did its written words took feathered form, took flight, became a great wheeling flock of birds, each one a purposeful song that filled the sky and filled the girl's heart with joy.

The great bird circled back and landed in front of the girl. Already, with its words singing in the treetops, it looked replenished, its feathers grown back in. "You did a brave thing, for the king will be very angry with you. How can I repay you? Name it."

"Oh no," said the girl. "You have brought birdsong back to the kingdom. That is all I need."

"Take this." The bird pulled a white feather and presented it to the girl. "With this quill your words will sing and your spirit will soar. And yes," the bird said as it flew away, "There will be pain."

The girl held the quill like a white flower; she held it like a sword; she held it as the key to her own escape.

THE THREE SISTERS

The three sisters spied it at once, a worn suitcase in their path.

"Unattended baggage!" the first cried.

"Abandoned," lamented the second.

"Lost," declared the third. "We should clear our path."

The first sister refused to go near the suitcase.

The second sister found the suitcase too heavy to manage.

The third sister found that she could manage to carry the suitcase and she set it upon a bench.

"We'll get blown to smithereens."

"I doubt it," said the third. "Look, there's a tag."

Contents may vary

"Hmmm," they intoned at once. Two of the three sisters agreed they should open it, the better to identify its owner.

The first sister moved some distance away with her fingers in her ears.

The second sister kept fumbling the clasp and found she could not open the suitcase.

The third sister studied the clasp and, on her third try, managed to unlock the suitcase.

"Don't lift that lid," pleaded the first sister.

"Yes, maybe we shouldn't look inside," wavered the second sister.

"We've come this far," declared the third sister. "We'll find out what is inside this suitcase that was in our path." She lifted the top of the suitcase.

When the suitcase was opened without incident all three sisters gathered round it to peer inside.

The first sister saw fear, all her fears from all her years, the little ones as well as the big ones. Some now appeared silly to her, looking in on all of them as she was, and she wondered if she might give some of them up. "Let's abandon this suitcase. Leave it," she suggested.

The second sister saw worry, all her worries from all her years, the little ones as well as the big ones. She saw they were a tangle and she wondered if she might unravel them or even give them up. "I agree. Let's leave this suitcase. We've no need for it or its contents."

The third sister saw wishes, hopes, and dreams. Some were from long ago, some forgotten, many she hadn't yet realized. Enthralled and distracted, she rummaged through the suitcase.

"Sister!" the other two finally yelled. "Let's get going. Don't you agree we should abandon this suitcase and its contents?"

"No! I'll take it."

But now the third sister found the suitcase clumsy to carry. She stopped often to review and examine its contents. Their progress on their path was slow. Finally she had to agree with her sisters. She sorted through the wishes, hopes, and dreams, deciding on what she might take with her and what she would leave behind in the suitcase. Shiny as the wishes were, she left them. Hope was light and easy to pack. All three sisters took hope from the suitcase and carried it close. The third sister then chose her biggest and best dream and wore it like a medallion over her heart.

The three sisters continued on their journey, their steps lighter and more certain.

RECKONING

Robert reckoned that the man sitting across from him on the train couldn't imagine anything worse than The Battle of the Wilderness. Robert allowed as how he'd fought in the Wilderness, then, feigning sleep, he closed his eyes on the questions, tried to close his mind to the answers, tried to bring his thoughts to the family farm, to his apple trees, to finally returning home.

But even now, on the train that chugged steadily north to Montpelier, his thoughts drifted back to his time after the Wilderness, returned to when he had worked in the field hospitals. There were indeed horrors greater even than those of battle; sights and sounds and smells that Robert sorely wished to forget. Robert wished to forget putrid air thick with the smell of filth and gangrene, ringing with the sounds of delirious men screaming and moaning; wished to forget gathering amputated limbs from the dirty blood soaked floor where they fell, stacking them like cordwood on the wagons or just chucking them in a pile outside the makeshift hospital.

Robert forgot how he'd left Vermont with his regiment four years back with a notion of returning as a man, a hero, for now he just wanted to run to his ma and his pa like a little boy waking from a nightmare, in need of comfort.

AFTER THE ELEPHANT

Robert was practically running now.

He would have missed sugar season, but his pa would appreciate his help with spring planting. His pa wouldn't ask him, as the man on the train had, about the Battle of the Wilderness.

Soon he'd be eating Ma's cooking, would tousle the hair of his baby brother, now a boy of six. He'd teach him everything there was to know, would have him driving the team, would set him up with his own team of oxen.

Robert ached to again work the farm, to mesh with the seasons.

Almost home; soon he would set this damn musket down.

SCION

Robert took up the fleece from its peg on the wall, the one from the big old ram, the one used to cover the seat of the sleigh in wintertime. He gently placed it over the Morgan's back explaining in soothing tones, "It's as much ta protect your back as my backside. I'm a lot more bones than the last time we rode up ta see Mary Eliza."

The last time had been almost four years ago, ostensibly to look over the apple orchard with Mary Eliza's father, but really to let them both know he'd be leaving with the Vermont 1st Infantry. Now, his satchel bristling with cuttings, he was again making the trip up the hill road on the pretense of checking on her father's orchard. The old man's orchard had seen great improvement in the time that Robert had begun to take an interest in Mary Eliza, before he had gone off with his regiment. But as he rounded the bend in the road, nearing the farmhouse of Mary Eliza's family, Robert saw that the orchard was again going wild, appeared to have been unattended in the time that he'd been gone.

From the front of the unpainted farmhouse three figures watched Robert's approach. It was the old man who spoke first, saying simply, "You're a might late, young man." Thinking he was referring to the apple scions, Robert replied that he thought they might still take but that there was a lot of pruning work to be done as well.

The old man spat on the ground, told Robert that all he ever needed from that orchard was cider apples, that it was fine just the way it was.

By now Robert had dismounted. He stood beside his horse, confronted by the sight of Mary Eliza standing with Elija Jones, a young man about his own age from a farm further up the hill road, a farm that had, even well before the war, been run down in all ways. Now here stood Elija, grinning awkwardly, balanced on a crude wooden crutch, his left leg gone below the knee, and, though it ended below the elbow, his right arm around Mary Eliza.

As if to explain, Mary Eliza said, "Elija needs me."

"But, I thought…" Robert trailed off, for he hadn't ever actually voiced his intentions. His eyes slid over the ragged orchard and the scrawny horse in the paddock by the barn and he had to wonder exactly what it was he had thought.

Robert fetched the grafting knife from his satchel. He used it to strip some pieces of rawhide from the edge of the fleece that blanketed his horse then cut off a broader piece, one that had a generous amount of soft wool. Robert helped Elija to lean against Mary Eliza while he bound the thick piece of fleece to the top of his crutch.

"That's much better, much obliged," Elija finally spoke, but Robert was already back on his horse, already turned around and headed back down the hill road to his own family's farm, his apple cuttings still bundled in his satchel.

HE SAYS

He sees himself as a harmless adventurer, a learner and a teacher. He says it's never about conquest.

He loves, he says, says love is a borderland, its borders permeable and transient, a place for walls to crumble, for barriers to come down, an exercise of dissolution, a pursuit of communion. He says each encounter is the coalescing of commonalities and of differences, exploring paths of shared experiences while discovering new paths that lead to new territories, unbounded.

Inevitably comes the withdrawal, the retreat behind invisible lines, one already looking to the next frontier, the other surveying the breach; taking stock, shoring up.

SEPARATION

She trailed her finger around his navel as she spoke. "My bellybutton."

"What?"

"That's the first scar we get, the first scar of separation."

"Ok," he said, rolling onto his side, "Besides your bellybutton, what other scars do you have?"

"The blankets when you toss them aside and leave my bed. A scar of separation."

"Really?"

"Yes, and when you go, it is wrenching. The door is a scar."

"Another scar of separation? Drama! I return, we heal."

"What makes you think I have scars?"

"Everyone does. They're our imprinted stories. I showed you where I slid into the barbed wire fence." He lifted his calf for her to see the scar again, then kissed her, held her gaze. "Thing is, we've been together a few times, but always with the lights off, always you wear a nightshirt." Her eyes dropped.

"Look. Pruning saw slipped the branch, ripped my finger."

She kissed his finger then pushed his hand away. She sat up, pulled off her shirt. "Scars of separation," she whispered. "But I got away."

"Know that I'll never hurt you," he said, gently tracing each raised imprint of the plunged knife.

RENDERED

"It's too tight," Marlie complained as her mother hurriedly strapped her into her car seat. Today she'd made her mother late because she'd been absorbed watching a moth ensnared in a spider web, hopelessly struggling, its wings rendered useless.

Craft time was underway when Marlie arrived. She quickly got herself some sticks and yarn too. Her thoughts swam in the colorful weave of her careful work.

"Nice dream catcher, Marlie. It looks just like a colorful spider web."

Marlie paused; loosened the yarn, undid each wrap and weave, dismantled her creation.

DISBELIEF

Me and Jimmy, we usually would go to the swimming quarry, an older quarry surrounded by trees and filled with deep clear water, but on this day we came up here to what we call Dry Quarry, a place cut into the side of the hill. There's a great view, which is one reason to climb up here, but we also just enjoy chucking pieces of granite from our high perch on the ledge over the cut and watching it disappear and then hearing it crash and shatter below on the shelf of granite at the bottom of the quarry.

I sat down when we got up there, just enjoying the view for a bit, and to be honest, the height does bother me. I like to sit down and get centered but Jimmy, fearless and surefooted even on that sheer ledge, you know how he is. Always in motion, he's already chucking rocks and gathering up a pile of them for when he's ready for a more methodical chucking.

I'll never in all my life forget what happened next and how it happened, and even though we have an English teacher who tells us try not to use clichés, sometimes things just happen a certain way and that's how it gets told. Like Jimmy stepping on those loose rocks that moved like marbles, Jimmy skidding backwards right over the edge into the air. It was like watching a cartoon. That English teacher, she also said something about a suspension of disbelief and that was the look on Jimmy's cartoon face, like he just couldn't believe he was in the air, and I swear he was suspended there just off the ledge in the air and like in the cartoons he seemed to believe that he might actually run on air or flap his way back to where I sat. But then, after that split second that seemed to last forever, it became apparent gravity would have its way, even with Jimmy. Still suspended in air, still looking at me, Jimmy seemed to know it too. He stopped flapping and flailing. He tried one more trick. He folded, kicking his feet up overhead, reaching his arms down, and descended in perfect dive form, as if the granite would part like water, would take him in and let him arc back up to break the surface, triumphant.

And this might sound cliché, but because of that time Jimmy stole a bunch of melons from that hippie market garden and we brought them up here to chuck, I can tell you from first hand experience that when his head hit it really did sound like a melon coming apart. I can tell you, the only thing that echoed against the granite walls was silence.

BURST

After Jimmy's dive ended at the bottom of the quarry, that awful silence echoed forever, washed right up and over the walls of granite, a massive wave of soundlessness that enveloped me where I knelt looking down to the quarry floor to see with my eyes that last thing I had heard.

As if viewing a movie I saw myself back away from the edge, still on hands and knees, saw myself crawl away to heave violently in the bushes, all without sound.

Then I was back in my body, picking my way back down the steep trail that Jimmy and I had climbed to the quarry ledge, all the while the silence a bubble around me so that I couldn't hear the insects that shrilled in the rising heat, couldn't hear my breath burning hot and heavy in my throat.

When I got to our bikes I had to untangle them, hating Jimmy for just dropping his bike, not caring that his handlebar got jammed in my spokes but there was no sound as I twisted and tugged and then in anger threw his bike back down before I pedaled furiously down the hill, trees peeling away in my wake, my eyes intent on the trail, my ears ringing with that awful silence.

I skidded to a breathless stop at my dad's shop and he rushed to me with a worried face. Then the silence thinned and I heard myself as if from a distance telling about the cartoon; about Jimmy slipping on the pebbles like marbles then treading air before diving headfirst into the granite.

My dad called 911 then held me tight to him, and at last I shed some tears, at last that bubble of silence burst. Wrapped in my dad's arms, I heard the sirens making their way up the old quarry road, heard the soothing lie in his voice telling me it was going to be all right.

ONE HANDED

Uphill or downhill, biking was the only thing I could ever best Jimmy at but since he wasn't there I chose to walk my bike up the steep trail that led off the old quarry road. This time I didn't bother to mash the pedals the whole way, to arrive triumphantly weak kneed and winded at the spot where I would have waited for him to catch up, where we would have both left our bikes to walk up to the ledge overlooking the dry quarry.

His bike was still there where he'd left it, where I had left it, chain side down, like I'd told him a hundred times not to do. I avoided even looking at the trails, the one going up to the top of the quarry, the other winding to its bottom. I would never take either of those trails again; I never wanted to see that place again.

But I would retrieve his bike, didn't want to leave it up there. I picked the grass out of his chain and cog, pointed both bikes down hill, mounted mine then coasted down the trail one handed while steering his with my left hand, a feat that Jimmy never mastered. I rode like that all the way down the trail, down the road through town, all the way to Jimmy's empty house.

I wonder what it would have been like to have gone to Jimmy's funeral but his mom, she said she couldn't even look at me, said she didn't know how I could have let that happen to Jimmy and I had no answer for her so here I was in his garage during the service cleaning up his bike, lubing the chain before putting it up on the wall rack, the spot where Jimmy's bike was always kept through winter.

I walked around the basketball that was still where we'd left it, got back on my own bike and pedaled home in the hot summer sun, taking the long way to avoid the church, taking the long way to put distance between me and that silent garage.

TRANSFORMATIONS

Since putting Jimmy's bike away on the day of his funeral I'd hardly left my room, hadn't seen anyone except my dad, so I was surprised when I heard him yell for me to come down, that I had a visitor. Clumsy yet curious under the pall of grief, I stepped into my jeans, pulled on a t-shirt, went downstairs and out onto the porch.

The last person I expected to see was Jimmy's mom, but there she was with an old backpack of Jimmy's. She looked so tired and not just because she hadn't done her hair or make-up like usual but she tried to smile at me and she said 'hey, I'm so sorry'. My dad gave her some coffee before leaving for the shop, before leaving us alone on the porch.

She was able to sip coffee, but me, I didn't move in that awful quiet, didn't know what to do or say, so I just waited while she drank coffee, waited until she put the mug down and asked me if I would go up there with her. She said she wanted to see where Jimmy and I were that day, wanted to see where it had happened.

We drove the old quarry road as far as we could in her car then walked to the trail that led up to the Dry Quarry ledge. She wore Jimmy's backpack but easily kept up, just behind me on that steep climb, and like Jimmy, she didn't plop down as I did at the top but immediately walked around, testing the edge, making me nervous.

She finally sat down between me and the backpack. Then she made me tell exactly how it happened and where, everything I remembered, and she got up and stared for the longest time down to the granite shelf below, stood right where he had last stood before slipping.

Her movements were more slow and careful than his but I was sure relieved when she sat down near me again away from the edge. She sat down with me and we both cried and cried right there, side by side, and she said it wasn't anyone's fault, said Jimmy was always careless, too much energy, no common sense, it wasn't anyone's fault.

When it seemed like we might be done crying she reached for the backpack, opened it up to reveal some of Jimmy's old toys, his Transformer collection. She said she'd planned to give them to me since me and Jimmy used to love playing with them so much but just decided I was too old now and that she couldn't bear the thought of me having to hang on to old toys that might only make me feel sad.

She stood up and looked at me with a grin that was so like Jimmy's, that gleam in the eyes, and said for me to get up, we were going to transform these toys. She emptied the backpack on the ledge and then Jimmy's mom and I chucked those Transformers as hard as we could down into the quarry, our cheers when they shattered echoing off the granite walls.

After, as I struggled to keep up with her back down the trail, I sure knew where Jimmy got it from.

NASHVILLE DREAMS

People come here to where the stars burned bright.

Stirring embers of memories, sifting through the ash

They're looking for Patsy, looking for Johnny Cash

Tourists ignore my singing, walk by my coin sprinkled case, go inside where it's warm, go inside for ten-dollar drinks, where they'll tip the band for playing lousy covers, tell them they sound real deal. Like they'd know.

They walk by, they look right through me, unseen space between the stars

Just another street bum, all I have is my guitar

Cold. It'll be another sleepless night of shivering, of wishing underneath the stars.

MOTHER CHURCH

Outside the Ryman, hoping for coffee, I watch an agitated couple. Seeing me, they hand me a ticket, say 'enjoy the tour', disappear up the street.

I'm happy to go inside, warm, with clean bathrooms. Not how I dreamed it, but I'm going to the Mother Church.

For hours I sit in the pews, awestruck. Memories and magic spirit the altar of the Grand Ole Opry stage. Tourists come and go but I remain, unmoving. I am moved. I am restored.

I leave, hopeful again. Looking up I see, high above this haunted town, a bald eagle soaring, searching.

COVERING

He almost bumped right into me on the sidewalk, a cell phone held to an ear with one hand, his other arm cradling a fiddle case, all the while striding rapidly down the hill towards Broadway. Suddenly he stopped and turned, I thought maybe to apologize, but he didn't say anything for a while, just looked me all over, me with my knapsack and guitar in its beat up case, he just standing there without saying anything long enough that I started to get edgy and move away, but then he asked could I play the classics.

I stood up tall and told him I could play fairly well, could sing too, knew the classics but didn't play covers.

"Oh, an artist, yeah, me too, I don't do covers either, except when I'm in need of a paycheck, and right now my guitarist is stone-drunk somewhere and I didn't know if you'd be interested in covering for *his* paycheck in forty-two minutes."

I told him if he could get me something to eat within forty-one minutes, and if I could perform just one of my own songs on stage, he had himself a sober guitar playing back up singer.

He laughed, said you never say no to your last resort or to your first real opportunity, and we walked together to the honkytonks on Broadway, carrying our instruments to the one where, in forty minutes, we had a gig.

LEARNING TO WALK

"You talk a lot," the girl said.

As they continued walking along the road she could not help considering the comment. Was it a criticism, a complaint? The girl had said it in her quiet cool tone, just another of her observations, always stated succinctly and as indisputable fact. So, after considering it some more she had to agree, all things being relative.

The girl was the daughter of an old friend. She had agreed to spend a couple of weeks here to be around during the day when her friend was at work. She could work on her writing, her friend had said. Her daughter wouldn't be a bother; she was very independent.

She hadn't hesitated, the timing was perfect for her, a chance to get away and yes, she would use the time to work on her writing. But from the beginning she was intrigued and distracted by the girl's activities, which seemed to involve a great deal of time outdoors. She asked the girl if she might join her. This request was met with a shrug, which she took to mean yes. So she often tagged along as the girl ventured to a particular pool in the brook or a clearing in the woods or a large rock where the girl might climb, or just sit in silence.

At the girl's behest she stopped wearing shoes. The girl had not given a reason why she should discontinue the use of shoes, had not expounded at all on the virtues of bare feet. She had simply said, "You should stop wearing shoes." Now as the afternoon sun shimmered through the whispering treetops they tread the smooth packed dirt road, their bare feet warmed with some steps, cooled with others in the dappled light.

"I guess I do talk a lot. Words are important to me…any job that I have ever had has had to do with communicating and writing…"

Her voice trailed off as she realized that she had already told the girl more than once about her career. The first time the girl had said nothing until she had finished explaining what it is that she does and how that came to be. Then the girl had paused and looked thoughtfully at her for a moment before responding, "Umm." And that was all. Now the girl didn't say anything. She kept walking just ahead of her at the road's edge, head bowed slightly towards the ground.

She was used to answering people's questions about her work, was accustomed to their inquiries. Maybe the girl didn't quite understand what she had been telling her. She tried to think of a way to explain things to this child. Maybe she would do a piece of writing for her, maybe some little piece filled with imagery about these woods that she seemed to enjoy so much, show her how one can express and communicate about things that one cares about. Maybe then the girl would at least lift her head up and look around more, even if she remained quiet.

As they walked on she looked around. She gazed as far into the woods as she could. Maybe she would see a deer. That would be good to write about. She looked up at the sky. Sometimes hawks soared overhead, but at this moment there were just a few high wispy clouds through the treetops. Even if she didn't see an animal like a deer or a hawk, one of those would work well. Yes, she would use a deer in her piece anyway. She was already thinking of ways of describing a deer in the woods. The girl was still walking in her peculiar way, her eyes sweeping the roadside. She would never see a deer, even if they walked right by one, the woman thought.

Suddenly her partner's words from their last argument flooded her mind. It hadn't started out as an argument. It had started as a conversation, the one that she always started, the one that exasperated her partner. *I'm here aren't I? You don't appreciate what's right in front of you!*

She yelped as her bare foot came down on a sharp piece of gravel.

"Look," the girl cried.

She looked far ahead. She looked deep into the woods. "What?"

"There."

She looked to where the girl was now squatting by the side of the road.

"It's just a newt." The girl smiled and explained, "If you walk carefully and keep your eyes open you never know what you might see."

Crouched down beside the girl she could smell the dampness of the roadside ditch, the moss, the ferns, the moldering leaves. The bright orange newt, no bigger than her pinky, stood in relief against the dusty gray road. She took in every detail of the newt, its black pinhead eyes, the red speckles on its side, its stubby toes and rubbery movements. She started to say something to the girl about how it was both delicate and tough; so intent of purpose. But she stopped herself. The girl already knew.

As they continued on towards the house, she did not look ahead to the bend in the road but instead she let her eye linger on the mossy stone, the unfurling fern, and the exquisite beauty of small things.

TEETERING

"Oh yeah! This party is just getting started!"

No one pays much attention to her husband's emphatic and very loud proclamation, because the fact is the party, a backyard barbecue, has been going on for quite some time. She notices the trademark wobbling and teetering. She knows the party is coming to a close.

Accepting his invitation to dance, she maneuvers him lurching and weaving to the truck even as she says goodbye to the others, even as he proudly slurs about how lucky he is to have a strong farm girl that knows how to take care of him, even as he makes specific suggestions towards that end.

"Don't start anything you can't finish, you old drunk," she admonishes him, even as he falls into open-mouthed snoring sleep.

The next morning, reaching for her hand, he manages to mumble, "We had a real good time, huh?"

"Don't even get me started."

BIG BREAK

I am no musician, not with these big meaty mitts, but I sure enjoy good music, like to go to that little pub where the acts set up right there in the corner, like to sit close at the nearest table to watch and listen.

This guy the other night, man he was something, just himself and a well worn but well tuned acoustic six string, and man! Well, like I say, I am no musician but he was something to hear and to see. He had these thick glasses half hidden by his tangled mop of hair, and I don't think he was seeing anything anyway he was so intent, just playing, his music amazingly clean and clear. He was versatile, as skillful a picker as I've ever heard, but my eyes ended up focused on his left hand, flowing up and down the neck of his guitar, his fluid fingers like nothing I've seen, wringing amazing sounds from that old Martin of his.

Pausing, mopping his brow, wiping his glasses, he announced that he had gotten a big break, had a recording contract and was heading to a major studio in a couple days. As he was doing all this his glasses slipped and skidded to a stop near where I sat. I think this guy can hardly see without his glasses because I had already picked them up to hand to him when he bent over feeling about for them on the floor, but I didn't expect that. I can't tell you how bad I felt when I heard the crunch of his left hand under my big dumb boot.

RECONCILIATION

The bear looked up when the door opened, saw her come into the bar, watched her decide where to sit. Those three brothers were crammed into a booth, as usual. Was that disdain he saw in her eyes for them? Because they were pigs?

She went to a booth away from the three pigs, sat down briefly. Too soft? She went to a high-top, clambered up onto the stool. Quickly got back down. Too tall? Finally she settled at the bar a couple seats down from him. He heard her sigh. Just right.

He must have been staring, for she glowered at him. "Do I know you?"

"We've met."

She hadn't changed much, older of course. Her golden locks, now shoulder length, had paled.

"Well I don't remember and I don't want to know you now." She ordered a drink, kept looking at the door in the mirror over the bar. Noticing, the bartender gently told her to relax, that the big bad wolf frequented a bar on the other side of town.

She laughed nervously, didn't say anything. She wasn't afraid of the big bad wolf, just had a long habit of looking over her shoulder. She scanned the room again and became doubly glad to not have sat at a booth. Why, she wondered, do people have to bring kids into a bar, when all she wanted was a quiet drink? It was a family of four, the mother tired and distracted, absentmindedly touching her short cropped blonde hair, as the boy and girl, twins perhaps, tussled and argued with each other while the father (not too bad looking even with his thick glasses) ignored them all. Finally she recognized the woman, despite the short hair. Rapunzel. She snorted; from one entrapment to another. She turned back to her drink. The bear was staring at her again.

"You don't remember me, do you?"

"I said I didn't."

"No, you wouldn't, you left in quite a hurry. After destroying our property."

"Oh… Baby Bear… all grown up. Look, that was a long time ago. Some porridge, a chair… I'll buy you a drink."

"You don't get it, do you?"

"What, were you traumatized by a little girl with golden locks?"

"Yes, actually, I was. Not so much by the damage you'd done, but by how my parents reacted. Or didn't react."

"What are you even talking about?"

"If the cops had come, who would have been questioned more, you, or the bears? I wanted justice and my parents just said to suck it up, let it go, don't start any trouble. You come into our neighborhood, enter our home uninvited, get into our stuff, breaking some of it, and *I'm* supposed to not start trouble."

"That's still not my problem."

"No, of course not. You just breeze through anywhere you like, no worries about being welcome."

"You don't know me."

"And you don't want to know me. You don't want to know that while my family and I were out for our walk that day we were alternately chased or run from for no other reason than we are bears. Like a bear can't walk in the woods. So our walks are secretive and stealthy; then we get maligned for being secretive and stealthy! I was already feeling so low that day and then to see that my home had been invaded…"

"I didn't know. I… I shouldn't have gone into your home, but I was running away, hiding out. I was scared, tired, hungry…"

The bear passed her a cocktail napkin. She wiped her eyes and blew her nose before continuing her tale. "My father had told some king a cockamamie story about me being able to spin straw into gold. In a classic lose/lose situation, if I actually managed that, then I was to marry the king."

"Wait… I thought that the king did marry that girl, but that she and her newborn escaped Rumpelstiltskin."

"No way. I mean that's the story, but what happened was I didn't want anything to do with either of them, the king or that other creepy little man. I took off running first chance I got. Been running ever since."

"Oh."

They sipped their drinks in contemplative quiet, ordered another.

"What was your father thinking?"

"I think he must have been speaking metaphorically, you know, telling the king I could make the most out of a bad situation, look on the bright side… But the king took him literally and I didn't have a chance."

"Greed, that's what does in poor people and bears, other people's greed."

"Got that right Baby Bear."

Their musing was interrupted as seven dwarves, still in their work clothes, noisily gathered at the bar.

She caught the bear's eye. "You wanna get outta here?"

"Yes, that'd be just right."

WORD WATCH

It was hard for him to catch everything she said, she talked so fast. When angry she talked even faster, emphatically, replete with innovative swear words. Just now she was on a creative streak. She was swearing mad. At him.

"Slow down," he pleaded. "I can't hear a word you're saying."

That got him an eye roll.

He didn't need to catch every word. He knew what he had said was wrong and was hurtful. They'd been talking about having a baby. He had signed that he hoped their baby wouldn't be born deaf.

That's when her fingers flew.

THE VISITANT

I have always tried to stay out of the way of the living. I have felt many people come and go, each claiming the house, the farm, as their own. Previous occupants, or at least their pets, have noticed me to some extent but we all just went about our own business, not interfering one with the other. I am the last of my own family and I just like being in this house, but I am not possessive of it; I've never minded sharing it.

When they first arrived, the woman, the man, the dog, I barely stirred. It had been a very long time since anyone had lived here in my house. Like the property, I was dormant, like a winter bear. I was content to remain in the corner of the parlor.

As this couple began settling in I did take an interest. I couldn't help it. There was an air of expectation. I felt the hope and the aspirations that they both brought with them. They seemed so happy with the farm, their prospects, each other. Over dinner they would talk about possible plans for the outbuildings and the property. They spent much of that first summer clearing the gardens and organizing the barn. They put wood up. They worked hard together inside and out making the place theirs and rescuing it from the ruin of long vacancy. I was pleased that they seemed content with the house as it was, which was not very different than it was a hundred years ago. I was eager for the energy that would be in my house again. It is a big house for two people. I wondered how long before they might have children, for they were yet young. I was pleased at the possibility of the farm being worked again, of children coming into the house and playing about the place. But they seemed to have other aims. They were taken with the farmhouse and the land, but were not farmers. They were, after all, people of letters.

The room that I prefer, the room that had been the parlor, where I had been laid out, she set up as her workroom, a place where she would write. He claimed an upstairs room as an office, as he was a college professor and also a writer. I have to admit this was something about which I knew little. None of my family nor any of the other occupants of the house had been bookish. I admired this couple's enthusiasm as they helped each other that first summer with small renovations and rearranged the old rooms to suit their needs, to make them into the spaces where they would pursue their ambitions. They brought in shelves for books, desks, a typeset machine- a typewriter she called it. I felt hopeful and proud of these young folk.

The leaves were just starting to turn when he started leaving most days for the college. Their breakfasts together were more hurried, though they would still talk about the gardens or have a request of one another; she might need something from town, he need her to search the unpacked boxes for his school shirts and ties. Talk of dinner, a quick kiss goodbye. Then she would settle into the parlor.

When she came into the parlor to sit down at her desk she disrupted my quiet. There was always a storm brewing around her. She cranked paper into that machine and pecked away. Though oft times it sat silent. She'd tap a pencil, make some notes, crumple them up, pick up the pencil again. Sometimes she would stay at her desk for long hours. Other times she would get distracted, would go work in the garden or read. When the machine sat silent she seemed to get angry or despondent. I became unsettled by her moods.

At dinner he would ask her how her day had gone. Her answers were brief and without detail; she tried to keep her anger and frustration from him, assured him that she was making some small progress, that she was content. He would brightly tell her about his day, some story about the students or his colleagues at the college. She listened it seemed, more out of duty than genuine interest. As the weeks went on, less and less did she ask for clarifications or details about the people and events of his day spent so many long hours and miles away. He stopped trying to get her away from her distractions, seemed distracted himself.

The days got shorter. The dinners in the dimly lit kitchen were darker too, with no conversation between them. He no longer asked her about her work; it had become awkward with her stilted responses. Sometimes he brought a book or papers to the table, hardly acknowledging her or the food.

Her efforts in the parlor were more agonized than ever with the unprofitable pencil tapping and intermittent pecking away at the typewriter. That typewriting machine seemed the key to her being content. I wanted her to be happy, wanted *them* to be happy, to feel the excitement that they had first shown for the house, the property. Each other. The arrival of this couple had awakened me, like a coal that was suddenly getting some air, glowing to life again. From my corner I just wished for her to be satisfied with her efforts as she struggled at her desk.

Maybe it worked. I felt her energy change. She still tapped the pencil, scribbled, tapped, but she seemed more focused, crumpled less paper. Between scribbling and working the typewriter she often stared towards my corner.

One evening she asked him to come look at my corner. The dog came into the parlor too, whined in my direction, left. The man stayed awhile, looking in my direction as he stood by her side. *Yes*, he agreed with her. *There's something there.* They talked about the corner, my corner; me. Apparently she had noticed me, had been aware of me for weeks, but was uncertain at first. *No*, she said, she *was not afraid. In fact*, she told him, she was *inspired, was finally unblocked in her writing*. He congratulated her, kissed her lightly on her cheek before returning to his upstairs office.

She spent more time in the parlor. More was pulled out of the typewriter; a stack of printed paper grew on her desk.

The days were getting longer. She was looking at seed catalogues, tried to talk to him about the garden over dinner. He was working long hours away at the college, often coming home late, sometimes well after dinner had gotten cold. For a while she waited dinner until he got in, when they would sit down at the table, push food around their plates in awkward silences. She eventually stopped setting the table, ate alone pacing in the kitchen if she ate at all. When he did come home he went directly to his office. Sometimes she followed him. Then there would be yelling.

Their anger haunted my house. I felt it. My corner was no longer the quiet refuge it had been for me for so long. I had awakened to these inhabitants, this couple, warmed to them, and now was unsure how to withdraw. I felt trapped.

One evening they had another couple over for dinner. Over these months, even as they were spending less and less time together, eating and sleeping separately, they still occasionally had guests. These dinner parties were sometimes successful ruses and diversions where wine was drunk and shared stories retold. On this night the act seemed to have run its course. She was more morose and upset than usual, was clearly distracted. Usually charming and gregarious with company, he barely spoke. The guests kept offering to help check on dinner; desperately prattled on amid the silences of their hosts. One thought to ask after me. *Was there still a column of light in the corner of the parlor, was it still her muse?*

She brightened and sat up. She told them how I was still there but that for the first time she was feeling uncomfortable sharing the parlor with me. Told how the dog absolutely refused to enter the parlor now. And she told them that she had a manuscript with the editor, that her agent was very encouraging. A novella, tentatively entitled *The Visitant*.

Finally the guests had engaged one of their hosts in conversation. But as she warmed to the topic of her success, he finally roused himself. He snorted derisively and loudly spoke over her to tell of his recently published journal articles. *Serious articles*, he insisted in a voice thick with drink. He disparaged her for writing ghost stories.

She tersely accused him of sleeping with the Dean. A silence stretched thin and brittle across the table.

The anger erupted with a loud clattering of dishes breaking. She says that I am responsible. I am not so sure that she didn't throw the first dish. But then dishes fairly flew off the shelves, dropping to the floor and smashing against the walls. Their guests tripped over themselves and the dog, as they scrambled out the door all at once.

When she tells it she says that after that evening "the visitant" disappeared. Just like that. She tells how she continued to live in the house, to work in the parlor but to never see the column of light or to feel the malevolence of that night again. For her it is the end of her visitant story.

He disappeared first. While she continued to yell and cry and dishes continued to break all around the kitchen, the man stepped out onto the night-dark porch, called for the dog and drove off. He came back two days later to get his clothes, said *I'm sorry*, said he could never give her what she wanted. *Except this house*, he said. And he left her alone. Alone with me.

She still writes. It seems to come more easily to her since the publication of the book. She seems, if not happy, resolved. She still comes into the parlor and sits at her desk most mornings. From there she looks to my corner, both warily and wistfully.

I am being careful. I'll not get drawn out again by this inhabitant of my house. She thinks I went away but I never left. I am still here and always will be. If she needs to feel the house is hers, I can wait. It's a blink in time for me. She's the visitant.

WEATHERCAST

The spell of summer is broken, its blue skies faded and grayed, awash on cloud-strewn winds. Trees champ and toss their manes as the winds rear and gallop. Leaves and small branches come unmoored, wildly skittering and wheeling about, ending in twisted, dreary piles, pelted by unrepentant rain.

The wind diminishes as night falls, though still mustering petulant gusts that usher the last of the clouds away, until, finally weary, the wind murmurs quietly in the silvered treetops. In the crisp light of a full moon, the night sky sparks and shivers.

Fall has come. Another spell has been cast.

SPELLBOUND

The spellbound are revealed

through their words and actions.

Their dark power of hatred grows daily

spreads, gathers strength,

consumes even as it is consumed.

The counter-spell must be found.

To fail is unthinkable.

Desperately we search

unsure of what the solutions could even be.

Magical potions?

Arcane rituals?

Mystical incantations?

Finally the realization-

the spell of hatred can only be overcome by loving words and actions.

The earth is my birthplace
all humans are my siblings.*

This we believe.

* Kahlil Gibran

THE QUILL'S MAGIC
ESCAPE

The king was angry, very angry with the sorrel-maned girl who had freed the great bird. The king was quite unused to being defied, of having anything taken from him, even things he had no right to.

"Throw her into the bird's stall," he commanded. "Melt the key in the forge."

The thin morning light that slanted through the barred window illuminated her tear as it dropped. Remembering the bird, the brave and stoic bird, she reached for the white quill pinned in her hair. Her tears would be her ink. No sooner had she dipped the nib into her own teardrop than she was transformed. As a small white bird she was able to flit through the window of the stall door. Unsteady with her wings, she perched on a shelf in the stable, uncertain of what to do next.

"The spell will wear off soon. Fly down from the shelf."

She fluttered to the straw-strewn floor and sure enough, as soon as she did, she was herself again, a girl holding a white feather, facing a sorrel horse that spoke to her over the half door of his stall. "Good timing," he said.

"But shouldn't the magic of the quill last forever?"

"The magic does last forever," replied the horse, "but do you really want to always be a bird? You're too young yet. You don't get out so easily. But I can help you with the next part of your journey."

As the kingdom was just beginning to rouse and attend each to their roles, the horse carried the girl rapidly away, she clinging to his mane, her own sorrel hair winging behind her. Finally the horse stopped in a wooded glade to rest. Only now did the girl ask how it was that a horse could speak.

"Every creature speaks."

"You know what I mean. I know horses. I have never known one to speak in human language."

"Tell me Girl, if you could, would you carry me?"

"Why of course I would, Horse." Then, before her startled eyes, the horse became a man.

"I was under a spell," he explained.

"Oh no. You're not a prince, are you?" she asked. For he was handsome and strong and stranger things had happened already.

"Ha! No, not I. I was a soldier once, in service to the king. When I was wounded he no longer found me useful. I was loyal, and thought that he would think kindly of those who had battled for him. I suggested that he, who has so much, instruct his royal physicians and magicians to take care of those soldiers who no longer rode to battle. He had his magician turn me into a horse to silence me. Until you came with the white feather I was unable to speak."

"I am glad you are not a prince. The king may not have use for a brave soldier, but I do."

Together they continued, she clutching the white feather, he clutching her hand.

EXTRACTIONS

After straining the rust he combined their gleanings. His children had become experts at extraction, at syphoning gas and oil from the abandoned and decaying automobiles. Their specialty was finding smaller machines that others overlooked. Lawnmowers. Leaf-blowers. Today they found almost five gallons of gas, three of oil. It was good but what was the current rate?

"I'll be back." His voice was husky and raw. Trading was dangerous. Yet necessary. His children watched him go.

He hoped for a good rate. Last time they were only giving a quart of water for each gallon of fuel.

SKY SIGNS

"Mommy, look at the sky. It's so pretty. Red sky at night, sailors' delight. Right Mommy? Tomorrow's gonna be a great day for our trip."

She grabbed up her little girl, held her close, told her yes, yes, it was going to be the best day ever, a wonderful trip.

"You're crying, Mommy. Is it because the sky is so beautiful?"

"Yes, darling, that's it, and you are so beautiful, and we're going to have such a great time."

It was not quite noon on a summer day. That morning they had listened to the birds' sunrise songs, had watched them disappearing in and out of the thick green-leaved tree canopy. Now in the black silence she held onto her child, so tight she could feel and hear her breathing, feel her heart beating against her own. Then sound returned; a rumbling buzz followed by a crushing roar that swirled the purple and orange sky roiling ahead of it, a massive thundering wave of color and sound that went unheard.

FEEDINGS

There are entertainments, of course, at the arenas. The Nation's Youth relentlessly root out books and paintings that still pollute many of the buildings. These fuel their great bonfires after the Feedings. Artists are kept on hand in miserable cells until a show at the arena. Here the large animals from the forsaken zoos finally get to satisfy their hunger.

The writers are among the first to go. Not just the journalists, but all writers, even poets and songwriters.

All eyes are on the pouncing tiger. Only the poet sees the single ashy page fluttering aloft on the wind.

ESCAPE

Sprawling from the impact of the tiger, the poet grasps at more loose pages from a half burned book of poetry among the bone-littered ash. The tiger nudges and paws her. The bloodthirsty spectators thunder in the stands, taunt the poet to get up and fight. Knowing that fighting for her life is futile, the poet fights for theirs. Even as the half-starved tiger rips and tears into her flesh, delighting the crowd, the poet stirs and claws at the ashes, releasing ninety-nine ragged edged poems to uncertain winds that carry them over the walls of the arena.

OPENING

The artist has witnessed many fires, many Feedings. Peering through the crack between two stones, he watches the poet stride purposely to where just the night before there had been a tremendous blaze of paintings, books, and the remnants of bodies.

The tiger is released.

The artist has seen many struggle desperately for their lives but this poet is much stronger. She conjures hope to rise up from the ashes.

He will go out in a blaze too. He finds a small sharp rock, begins cutting an outline of a phoenix on his torso, prepares for his upcoming exhibition.

LICKED

On his fourth birthday his dad went to prison.

Shortly before his eighth birthday his dad was paroled.

His mom and dad partied together until she od'd.

The man called Dad left them; left him, alone.

He searched the house in vain for hidden presents.

He found needles, empty bottles, and some uneaten oreos.

He ate in silence, imagining that she only slept.

Twisting each oreo apart, licking the filling, he knew.

This wasn't birthday cake and his mom wasn't asleep.

On TV, 911 calls bring help, action, and noise.

He would call when the oreos were all gone.

HANGTIME

In the hang-time of late fall, after leaves and before snow, out on the playground where the real schooling happens, mastery is measured in marbles. Rex's ragged bag is always full.

At morning recess Rex takes the ice out of the marble holes barehanded, then expertly bores the holes with the heel of his tattered Converses, making the holes smooth and sloped just so. Rex calls the shots; maybe boots and shoots, hitsies, no toesies… He always calls keepsies. There's no shame in losing to Rex. Sometimes a kid might even win a couple of rounds but then is obliged to accept the challenge of playing puresies or boulders, a higher stakes game he is certain to lose.

Rex has never been in the habit of gratuitously punching anyone but he will give anyone who suggests that he has a dog's name five good reasons not to make that mistake twice. Everyone that's anyone, that is anyone from around here, knows better; knows that Rex means king, and the king of the playground is always respected.

Most of the legends about Rex are true, including that he has never cried, not once, not ever through all of school, not even back in kindergarten when his dad was taken away. So out of respect everyone rushes to the swings or the slide on the Mondays after visitation, the mornings Rex's eyes water in the cold air. Then he stands alone, his marble bag heavy in the pocket of his thin jacket.

SCORING

Second term had begun. In the teacher's lounge they spoke of Robin as if the woodshop teacher wasn't even in the room, expressing surprise, disappointment even, in her class selections. Because of their daily talk he knew that Shop was an uncharacteristic choice for his new student; that she had been increasingly less academically inclined, was no longer involved in sports or afterschool activities.

The woodshop teacher didn't need to hear colleagues' comments to recognize that Robin wasn't the typical disenchanted and disenfranchised doper that he usually got in his classes. He made sure to give her challenging projects, encouraged her to be creative. Today he showed her how to use the table saw, reminded her to measure carefully before cutting. He was impressed by her interest and her questions, smiling with her at her delight in the word *kerf*, which she defined as being "the nothing that is left that is bigger than the cut itself".

"I want to score a design in my table top," she said. "Beautiful kerfs for all to see."

He agreed, gave some procedural advice, insisted that she roll up her customary long-sleeves. He was more surprised that she readily did so than by the meticulous scoring on her forearms.

ASPIRING

She didn't like when people argued with her, told her she should have greater ambitions. She knew what she wanted; she wanted to have a baby. She would tell the baby, "You are mine, mine, mine." She would be married to the baby's father and he would also say to the baby, "You are mine, mine, mine." She knew, even if she was only fourteen years old, that these were decent aspirations; knew that was a good way, the right way to raise a baby. She knew because she was still in the same State home where she had been abandoned fourteen years ago; she knew how it should have been. Now, partway to her goal, she smiled softly, hands on her belly, whispering, "You're mine; you are mine, mine, mine."

EVER AFTER

Once upon a time there was a princess born to a queen and king and raised in the manner in which princesses were raised. She grew up within the protective confines of a castle knowing always that she was awaiting a prince. Until the time of the arrival of the prince there was little that was expected of her other than to be a good girl, a necessary requirement for any princess. She did not wander the woods because she was told not to. She knew the stories. The woods were dark and dangerous, a place of trickery and temptation; no place for a princess.

The princess had a harder time with the rule against going to the fields. "Mother, why can't I go out beyond the moat to see what is happening in the fields? From the wall I see the people. There are children! Why can't I do what they are doing?"

"No! No, my dear, those are peasants, coarse, dirty, and ignorant. We provide them land and protection. They provide us food, which they grow. You are to understand that they have their place as we have ours. Promise me you will not have anything to do with them."

"Yes, Mother."

But often the princess watched the peasants from the castle wall, listened enviously to the singing and jovial shouting as the people harvested grains and vegetables, wondered at the skill and accomplishment of putting food on her table.

Peasant women worked in the castle kitchen. Though told how improper and vulgar these women were, the princess sometimes snuck in, lured by the good cooking smells and by sounds of laughter. She had never seen her mother or the other ladies laughing as these women did, holding their bellies, mouths open, wiping their eyes, their noses as they caused one another to snort and chortle with their commentaries. She knew such behavior was crude, knew that she could never join in nor indulge in such laughter herself.

Because this is a tale that happened once upon a time there is somewhere a witch. The witch too was off limits to the princess for the obvious reasons. So imagine the princess' surprise when she happened upon the witch outside the queen's chamber. The witch too was startled to be discovered but recovered her composure quickly.

"You're the witch!"

"Clever girl. You're the princess."

"May I ask you a question?"

"You just did. I will not tell you any more than you already know my dear. You know that you are the princess and that one day suitors will come. One will prove himself worthy, passing whatever tests your father subjects him to, returning triumphant after many adventures. Then you and he will marry."

"And we will live happily ever after?"

"I'll say no more than is already known. I am not involved in this particular tale. This one is all about the prince's quest though the details of his adventures need not be bothered with. There are plenty of tales already about the amazing feats of brave and clever princes."

"Then why are you here? Who are you?"

"I will not tell you more." The witch slipped quietly away down a back stairwell.

The princess became a young woman. Suitors came and went. Each was assigned tasks of great difficulty. None were capable of the Herculean labors that they eagerly set off to complete. The princess enjoyed the attention of the suitors and the excitement around their missions but mostly was grateful for the delay that their futile and failed endeavors afforded. She was becoming apprehensive, for happily ever after was never well defined, was it?

Then one day there came an appropriately handsome, perfectly polite prince whom all were sure would be capable of succeeding. All were correct. The time of this one's high adventure was the only delay left between the princess' present and her future, her happily ever after. While awaiting the prince's triumphant return there was increased activity among the peasants. More food was gathered and prepared; more wood cut and laid up. Though it meant more labor there was excitement in anticipation of the coming feasts and festivities. There was loud unrestrained laughter in the kitchen, in the fields and huts.

"Mother, why are you so silent? You never leave your chamber. Mother, soon I am to live happily ever after."

"Oh, child. I know. I know." Leaning on her velvet pillow, the queen stared languidly through the barred window of her tower chamber. She did not notice the princess slip out.

"Father," the princess said to the king, "Did you go on a quest to win mother's hand?"

"Why yes my dear, I did. I have told you. I slayed giants and dragons. I had to outwit many wily characters and creatures, proving myself to be clever and virtuous and able to keep my betrothed safe from harm."

The princess wanted more of the story but on this day the king was gloomy and withdrawn, lost in his own thoughts, so the princess left him alone. The king's thoughts were back on his long ago quest. He could not speak his thoughts to the princess, to anyone. He could not say that his quest was the only time in his life that he had felt alive. He could not say he hadn't wanted the adventure to end. He knew that the heart of the young man who would wed his daughter did not belong to her. He knew the prince was not driven by a desire to return to the princess, but was driven by the adventure, anxious to prove his bravery. "A princess is a poor prize after such times," thought the king. "A fine purpose, but a poor prize, for she is the end to manly living." The king only hoped that this prince was a better man than he. For it did sting that having proved himself worthy so long ago with valiant achievements far afield, he had done nothing since for the queen, a silent woman who cared nothing about dragons or giants. Perhaps he had in fact failed.

You know what happened next. The prince came back with his merry men amongst great fanfare. He had bravely crossed mountains, solved riddles, slain fierce and cunning giants. The hand of the princess was won. There was a wedding ceremony with a great many guests attending the celebrations and feasting. Finally the celebrations ceased, the guests returning at last to their own manors.

The princess also went away. Sitting in her coach she turned but could not see her parents who had each retired already to their respective chambers. The princess did not reward with smiles and waves the peasants who lined the road to see the procession. Slumped in her curtained coach she did not notice the inscrutable witch who watched from the edge of the forest. The prince rode ahead, to protect the princess he said, to ward her from harm. She could hear him retelling tales of his quest to the other men, heard their laughter even as she wept. She had known that this day would come, this day of leaving the castle of her childhood. She did not know what might happen next. She felt lost and helpless. The princess wept because she was beginning to realize that happily ever after was not just a long awaited moment but was a spell that she would be under for a very long time.

Behind the barred window of her chamber, wracked by undefined regret, the queen also wept, but she often did.

Alone in his chamber the king was surprised and overcome by the depths of his sorrow, realized at his daughter's leave taking. He too wept. He wept for the queen, the silent and estranged woman who had once been his princess. He even wept for the prince, his youthful rival and ally who had finally come and who, dazzled by his own success, could not yet see that loss attends every triumph and every gain.

The wedding procession wound out of sight. The peasants returned to their chores. The witch disappeared into the darkening wood. In the castle, quiet stole in to replace the din of the wedding celebrations, except in the kitchen, where remained a resplendent mess. Here raucous laughter rang out amongst the kettles and the plates. Working together, cleaning up after the royal and noble guests, the boisterous servants were unaware that the masters and the mistresses were silent and alone.

DARK OF WINTER

People joked that they walked on water that winter. Everywhere was frozen water. It came down as freezing rain and remained frozen, the countryside encased in a glassy sheen. Rain would be followed by a cold spell, with never any snow to soften the bleak monotonous gray. It was a winter of impossible travel, of long days indoors, of boredom with its attendant drinking and tempers. It was a winter when heinous occurrences, mute secrets, were blamed on the entrapments, the relentless icing.

She wished the crystalline memory that gripped her, frozen, would shatter, would melt.

PACKING

Sighing, Miranda looked through her closet, as if something new might have appeared. She finally took down the tired slacks, blouse, and sweater that she usually wore on Wednesdays. They would serve, though they'd serve better if she hadn't packed so many pounds around her middle.

So much besides her weight had changed since she began teaching; demoralizing and depressing changes.

Sighing again she adjusted the accessory that now completed her outfit. Her concealment holster used to tuck more easily into her waistband. Now the gun, like her dispiritedness, was harder to conceal.

WOLFMAN

Once upon a time we lived under one roof. Finally you left but sometimes, not very often, you return. Back for a visit you want it to be like old times. In front of our mother, the children, the grandchildren you start. Remember the time…

Your wife, she might have seen me tense, my breath tightening. Maybe she saw me raise my hands slightly, involuntarily. Did that happen? Did she see it if it did?

What you want me to remember with you, did that really happen?

Remember the time you say, when we were walking at the bottom of the field…

A common path; which time?

…and we saw the wolf.

Oh, that memory of yours. That time. You claim to have seen a wolf.

I remember exactly where we were when you claim to have seen it. Not far from the seasons strewn stonewall that marks the blurring boundary of overgrown field and damp softwoods, right at the spot where the trail leaves the sunlight and twists into the dark of thickening hemlock and balsam where we might have paused to let our eyes adjust.

I do not contradict your sighting even though it would have been, would still be, unusual. But now, in front of our mother, the children, the grandchildren, I will not agree to having seen your wolf too. I do not tell why I wouldn't have seen your wolf even if it were there.

I wonder; did your wolf make you defensive? Did you become instantly alert, did your vision narrow and focus that you might read the wolf's face, its body language, its mood? Were you anticipating its moves, ready to minimize the damage it might inflict upon you? Notice I didn't say ready to fight, or even suggest fleeing, for what chance with either tactic does one have against a wolf?

I do not know what you saw. I know well what I saw. I saw you stepping farther into the dark woods. I, expected to follow, remained at the edge of sunlight, the field at my back. I was alert, my vision, as always, narrowed and focused, my eyes on you, watchful, waiting to see if you would lope off or if you would attack.

Ask me again if I remember the time we saw a wolf. I did see a wolf. I think your wives and children have seen it too.

SEASONS

Jerod, still in funeral clothes, stood uneasily in his father's kitchen, in Judy's kitchen.

"No, Jerod, that four wheeler weren't his to give. You remember we got it when your dad had that DUI and we registered it in my name. I'll be keepin' it. Unless you wanna trade me for it. Seven cord dry wood."

Jerod thought maybe he remembered something about a DUI but he wasn't around much then. He met Judy's steady gaze for a while, trying to read her. He couldn't say for sure when or how the four-wheeler actually came to be here at Duffy's place. Finally he looked away.

"Aw shit, I ain't gonna argue with you over that old piece of crap. I just figured since he was my dad and all and you don't need it." Without a goodbye Jerod strode briskly to his truck and sped away up the driveway.

Judy let her breath out slowly. The lie had seemed effortless, but now she trembled as if she had just stood down a bear. Now that Duffy was gone she was just so uncertain about everything. She felt that she should be careful. She was afraid that Jerod would lay claim to Duffy's trailer-home and then she'd have no place to go. It was bad enough to be this late into the fall, winter really, with no wood put up. She did need the four-wheeler because what she really needed was firewood and she might be able to skid some windfalls out of the woods with it if the snow stayed off.

Judy figured the snow would stay off. Duffy had predicted it would. Duffy had always known when the ice was going to be out and when sugar season would start and end. Duffy had been locally acclaimed to be more accurate than the Farmer's Almanac. Last spring, before his diagnosis, Duffy had predicted a mild summer and fall followed by a winter like they hadn't seen in thirty years. No snow, but some real cold spells. People were recollecting Duffy's prediction now. The bit of snow that had fallen was a dry cold dust blowing over the tops of bare yellowed grass. It was cold and felt colder without the usual snow cover. Wood should have been put up, but Duffy had preferred fishing with his buddies throughout the summer, even as he got steadily thinner and weaker. Judy had never been too bothered by Duffy's fishing or by his knack for working just enough to get by, but before he had always been prepared for winter. This past summer she hadn't been able to talk to him about a winter that he wasn't likely to see. She hadn't reproached him for living as fully and happily as he could in the time he had left.

Judy slipped into her wool jacket and stepped out into the yard when she heard Gill's truck. Gill didn't even think to knock at the door of the trailer, just got out of his truck and went right into the shed where Duffy kept his machines and tools. He looked startled but not guilty when Judy asked him what was he doing as he loaded the chainsaw into the back of his truck.

"Oh, hey, Judy. I'm just takin' some of Duffy's tools. You know. 'Cause he'd want me too." Gill walked back to the shed.

"My god, Gill, I need that chainsaw. Look! There ain't barely a cord of wood there, what's left from last winter. It's December. I need wood."

Gill turned back, framed in the doorway of the big-beamed shed, unwittingly ringed by the blood and gristle that stained the ground underneath where the deer had hung and been dressed. And the moose. Judy wondered if any of that meat had made it into the freezer. Always a generous friend, Duffy had been even more so as his health deteriorated. "You can stay with me. I've got wood."

Judy studied Gill. Sometimes he could be lewd, but usually just ignorant. "Thank you, Gill, but Duffy meant for me to carry on here with this place. So I'll need that chainsaw. To cut wood."

"Oh, okay, sure." And Gill nodded and shuffled thoughtfully back to pluck the chainsaw out of his truck. He put it back on the shelf in the shed then returned. He leaned on his truck for a bit, gazing wistfully at the trailer, the overgrown yard and field, and the woods beyond.

"That Duffy. He was something."

"Yup. He was."

"Well, Judy, I'll be goin'." Judy shivered watching his tail lights disappear in the dimming late afternoon light, wondering if she had in fact just lied again. It felt like a lie because she knew that Gill was right; Duffy would want his friends and his son to have anything they wanted of his. Duffy hadn't said anything to her about what she should do, but surely he didn't mean for her to freeze. Hadn't he tuned and sharpened that saw for her?

Ever since Duffy had learned he was going to die, things started going his way, one lucky thing after another. Not that he was unlucky before. But after he got notice of his own dying, Duffy became more aware of his good fortune, and was grateful, appreciative of any little stroke of serendipity.

His friends were apprised of his observations and were enjoined to share in his luck. If Duffy noticed that it was a god given great day for fishing, they went fishing. And they caught fish, fish like they hadn't seen in years. Judy figured it was more than luck, that they were bound to be successful with the amount of time they put into it. Duffy hadn't worked since his diagnosis, and his working friends were taxing the patience of their bosses, the self-employed letting a lot of jobs go. "Carpe diem," Duffy had said. "I ain't innerested in no dang carp," Gill had answered. "I only eat perch or trout."

Duffy would be lucky to make it through the rest of fishing season, his doctor told him, certainly wouldn't be ice fishing. Duffy allowed as how he could let ice fishing go anyway, but that he was going to go six months at least, not the four that the doctor predicted. Duffy scoffed when the doctor surmised that he probably wanted one more Christmas. Christmas didn't matter. But deer season did.

As luck would have it, deer season came early for Duffy, was as he said, super-sized that fall. Soon after his diagnosis he found out that he had been drawn for a moose permit, a first despite applying every year.

Duffy's luck had changed. And the tag was for this sector, so he could hunt right out back where the moose were all through the woods and swamp. By the time moose season came around Duffy had had so many great fishing days and such luck throughout bird season, that no one was surprised when just two days in he got his moose. Duffy wasn't surprised. He was grateful to the moose that just lumbered across his path and graciously dropped almost immediately instead of having to be trailed through the alder and into the swamp where dragging him out would be hard labor for a healthy man. As it was, Duffy relied on his friends to help field dress and drag the giant animal while he mostly leaned against a tree, watching with labored breath. Even then he was buoyant with gratitude for the moose, for his friends, for the skim coat of snow that day that made the dragging easier for them, and for the sheer beauty of these woods. He breathed deeply. Then he coughed violently, painfully, staring at his boots, his hands on his knees. Finally he straightened to see the concern in Gill's eyes. "I'm alright. Just breathed too much in at once. Gawd, what a shot, huh? He just dropped for us. Lucky."

After the moose, Duffy rested up for regular deer season, staying around the house more, sleeping often. When he was up he was on the phone, leaving messages on his son's voicemail. Judy saw that Duffy was bothered, and didn't ask about these calls. Then one day she came home from work to see an almost new pickup in the yard. She carried groceries into the house to find a young man sitting in the kitchen, talking with Duffy.

"Hey, Judy, look who's here." Judy could only notice how Duffy beamed and even seemed healthier looking than he had that morning so she put aside her feelings for his son.

"Hey there, Jerod." She got dinner together while the father and son planned their hunting like nothing was wrong. Like things hadn't been terribly strained since Jerod and his mother moved out of Duffy's life over twelve years ago. Father and son talked hunting strategy like Duffy wasn't terminally ill and like Jerod didn't live three hours away, hardly ever getting together with his father. Duffy would add this reconciliation to the top of his list of good fortune.

"Judy, Jerod got a promotion at his work. He's doing real good."

And for that Duffy seemed especially grateful, relieved to see that his son was healthy and working a good steady job, even if it was way off in the southwest corner of the state.

"Got a new truck," affirmed Jerod. Duffy smiled, coughed, but recovered quickly. Jerod glanced apprehensively at Judy, who gave nothing away as she tended to her cooking. She pressured Jerod to stay for dinner.

All through dinner Duffy laughed and told stories. Somehow he gathered enough material from the limited times that father and son had spent together to knit a seamless narrative of adventures and good times, mending the tears and covering the spaces with his recollections, artfully moving around the darker times, tactfully leaving out the characters that had led Jerod away. Judy felt protective towards Duffy as he retold a past not wrought with pain and heartache. Jerod listened intently, the young man taking in Duffy's memories, now remembering them that way too.

Finally Duffy ran out of material and paused, worn out from the long stint of talking. Jerod seemed reluctant to go. "I have to get back for work, but I'll be back next weekend for deer huntin', Dad."

"Okay, son, see ya then."

As soon as Jerod was out the door, Duffy sagged, exhausted. Judy pretended not to notice, like she pretended not to notice that meals now for Duffy was food getting pushed around the plate, small little bites taken to be polite, swallowed with difficulty. The ketchup and salt and pepper on the lazy-susan in the middle of the table were crowded by brown pill bottles. Duffy took some as he sat for a while in silence.

"That was some nifty patchwork there, Duffy."

"You don't think he's just pitying a dying old man?"

"Nah. And you ain't old."

"Won't ever be old either."

Judy helped Duffy into bed, and lay with him. "I'm a lucky man," he said, groggy with sleep. She held him as he fell asleep, even though the dishes were still dirty in the sink.

Duffy slept a lot that week before opening day, but when Jerod arrived Friday night Duffy was sitting up, sharpening his knife, his deer rifle freshly cleaned, lying bolt open across the table. He helped his son get set up for sleeping on the couch. There was little talk as the plan was to wake early.

"See you in the morning son."

"You, me, and Gill."

"Yup, that's the plan."

"See ya in the morning, Dad."

Judy only worked till noon on Saturdays. Gill's truck was still in the driveway, along with Jerod's. She wouldn't have been surprised to find the men at the table, eating, maybe having a beer, but when she went in the house was empty and by the looks of things they hadn't come in for a break. Judy kept busy around the house but was increasingly nervous as the afternoon wore on. Finally, well after sunset, she heard the men stamping their feet up the steps. They filed in, leaning the rifles in the corner by the door.

"See anything?" she dutifully asked. All three looked happy and healthy, red cheeked under their hats.

"Ah, there was all kinds of sign out there. And a doe and skipper crossed in front of me," said Gill. "Your man Duffy claims he let a four pointer walk on by, but I think he just choked or somethin'."

Duffy just smiled at his friend. "Oh, I coulda dropped that one but it was too small. Who wants to be all done on the first day of deer season anyway? I gotta feelin' about this season. Remember I told you about that big boy way up the ridge?"

"Yeah, well, a deer in the hand is tastier than the one over the ridge."

They'd spent a long day in the woods. Judy waited until the other two men were washing up for dinner before asking Duffy how he was feeling. "I feel good. Really. We had a real good day and the fresh air and sun felt good. Don't worry about me, Judy."

Judy of course worried, but Duffy and Jerod continued to hunt hard all week. Gill had to go back to work after the weekend, leaving the father and son to hunt alone. They continued to get out at daybreak, usually not returning until after sunset. Both father and son felt they were getting to know the legendary ridge runner. Though they hadn't actually seen him they saw sign and were re-strategizing specifically for this buck. Judy watched them as they sat at the table rehashing the day and planning the next. Duffy was beaming. The awkwardness between him and his estranged son was gone. Duffy insisted he was feeling better and stronger with each day of hunting.

"He really is all cleaned up, Judy. He really is. He handles himself real good in the woods too."

"That's great Duffy."

"It's great all right."

They lay together in bed, the light still on. Jerod was on the couch in the living room watching TV. He would be returning to work and his own home after the weekend. "Think you'll get that deer?"

"Ah, Judy, as lucky as I am, do you have ta ask?" Then he was fast asleep. Judy watched him for a while before reaching over him to switch off the lamp. His bedside stand was laden with medications. Duffy had moved them from the lazy-susan before deer season started, partly she believed because he was embarrassed by them but also because he did not want to tempt Jerod with the array of bottles. Judy wasn't even sure what all the pills were or were supposed to do. She suspected that Duffy wasn't taking many of them. From the beginning he had disagreed with the doctors on most things, filling the prescriptions just to make them feel better. Once home, he took only the pills that made him feel better.

"These other ones," Duffy had said, "These're supposed to make me live longer, maybe like a day or two or maybe a month but then I would feel like shit and look like shit. If they ain't gonna cure me- well, shit. Besides, my woman has always loved my long thick hair." He had squeezed Judy to him, playfully putting his hair in her face.

Judy continued to lie awake beside Duffy. She wondered if she should have tried harder to argue with him regarding treatments. After one surgery that only revealed more bad news, he refused further surgeries. He refused chemo and radiation. His reasoning was that they couldn't guarantee the same time return that all those treatments would require of him while he was still fit enough to enjoy the life he had remaining. So began his lucky streak. Now he was already a couple of months past what the doctor had said was likely. He didn't just make it to deer season; he was hunting, with his son. Every day, going way back in the woods, walking for miles, getting stronger and feeling great. He said so. Maybe, Judy thought, maybe his luck would hold.

Judy got up with the hunters early Saturday morning. Gill arrived while she made breakfast and coffee. Gill and Jerod spoke easily over breakfast, Duffy smiling over his coffee. "Today's the day," he said.

"Yeah, we'll see," said Gill. "Just don't you get all buck feverish and screw things up. You wanna switch that rifle for a shotgun with buckshot, just in case you do see one?"

"You know," Duffy said to Jerod. "It's one thing to teach a son to hunt, a good thing. Remember when I taught you when you were nine, ten years old? But, my gawd, every year I have to teach this guy how to hunt. Over 'n over. He just ain't learnin'. And he ain't gettin' any younger."

"None of us are. Let's get going."

Judy watched them go out into the early morning dark.

63

After work Judy got groceries and ran errands. Even with her later arrival she didn't really expect the men to be home, had gotten used to their after dark returns all week. She hadn't expected to see two large buck hanging in the shed doorway either, but that's what greeted her when she turned down the driveway. Jerod's truck was gone. Inside on the kitchen table was a note. 'I'm over the Moon', he'd written. That's what Duffy used to say when he wanted to go to the Blossom Moon for drinks and dancing. 'Let's go over the Moon'.

They had met at the Blossom Moon. It was her first time there. Traveling through, Judy didn't know anyone, had stopped on impulse. Duffy introduced himself as soon as he saw her, treated her as if she was an expected guest. She didn't get drunk with Duffy; he was already drunk. They danced once but it was a sloppy struggle and he gave up. She drove him home because he asked her to and he was drunk and she wasn't. She helped him into his house. He stumbled to his bed, begging her with slurred speech to join him. She did. He fell asleep almost as soon as he lay down with her, fully clothed, in his arms. The next morning she woke first. She made breakfast for both of them, as she did every morning since. Every night since that first she had fallen asleep in his arms.

The Blossom Moon was lively when Judy arrived. There was a good crowd. All there had heard of the two big buck getting shot in the same morning in the same push. Gill and Jerod were beginning to show the signs of the other patrons' generosity. Duffy smiled at Judy.

"Hey Judy! Did you see Jerod's deer?"

"What about my deer? Jeezus, Duffy."

"Jerod's is bigger."

"Size don't matter, you of all people should know that. Besides, 202 pounds? Eight point rack? Oh, yeah, buddy. Oh yeah."

"But Gill, mine's a nine pointer, 212 pounds. Yours is just a skipper compared to my deer."

Judy watched the men banter, Duffy grinning away. "What happened to your lucky streak? No deer for you?"

"This is the luckiest day of my life. It was great hunting. I put those guys right where they needed to be then pushed those deer right to 'em. Who knew there're two of those big boys up there? I could'a gotten a shot off, but I seen that nine pointer was headin' right to Jerod and 'at he'd have a surer shot. Besides, I 'ave gotten plenty of deer... You should'a seen these two. It was perfect. Great day. Ah, Judy, my luck is just fine."

Judy watched Duffy. He was having a great day, had had a great week, and she hoped that maybe his luck would hold. Surely he couldn't have faked the show of strength that those two deer, that these two men with him now, had required of him. Duffy was still just beaming and smiling, getting as much or more credit for the kills than the shooters, even as he tried to redirect the praise towards them. She also noticed that he leaned heavily on the bar, wasn't the animated hand and arm talker that he usually was. She noticed that Duffy was given many free beers but that he deftly managed to provision others with those beers, unnoticed by all but her and the bartender, who exchanged a quick but worried look with her. The crowd at the Blossom Moon was oblivious to any weakness in their friend. "Doctors don't know shit" was a repeated mantra around the bar as people celebrated Duffy, his hunting season, and his apparent good luck with his health.

"Jeezus, Duffy, there's still a whole other week. What'd you save for yourself?"

"Oh, I think these're the best deer we'll see from around here for a while. Anyway, I got things to do this week, don't think I'll hunt too hard. I'm happy to have hunted with Jerod and of course to help out old Gill, here. Maybe these boys will put a hunk or two of that meat in my freezer, I'll be all set."

"Hey, Duffy, what are you'n Judy doin' for Thanksgiving? You're welcome to join us." Many people mentioned Thanksgiving to them that night. Judy listened for Duffy's response. She was relieved but worried too when he declined. "Ah, Judy and me, we wanna just lay low this Thanksgiving."

That's what they did. By Thanksgiving, five days later, Duffy was back to the bad coughing spells that left him exhausted. He kept his friends off, told them to let him rest up for a bit then they'd go ice fishing, by gawd. Judy was putting in fewer hours at the store, but when she was there she heard the rallying cries throughout the rumor mill, that Duffy was getting well, that Duffy was planning on ice fishing with Gill and the boys. "That doctor don't know shit. He don't know Duffy." Judy honored Duffy by not refuting these hopeful sentiments, though at home both she and Duffy knew without speaking of it that he would not be fishing. Judy quit the store altogether.

It was an ordeal for Duffey to walk from the bed to the couch but he insisted on that morning ritual. Judy made it seem natural for her to support him as he walked, to wait with him as he coughed, caught his breath midway. Once to the couch Duffy would rest, maybe even doze, while Judy got the Mason jar that would save him a trip to the bathroom. Then she sat with him. Holding hands, they would quietly talk or not talk, or Duffy might add to his catalog of good fortune and serendipitous events.

"My dad would've loved to have seen those deer, to've seen me and my son bring those deer in." Duffy coughed, paused, regained his breath before speaking again. "You never got to meet him. He'd be real happy for me, having a woman like you."

Duffy coughed again, wincing with the pain of it. Judy tried to spare him by speaking for him. "I know what you'd say to your dad, Duffy. You'd say, 'This here's Judy and I'll fight for her but not with her.'" He kept his eyes closed and Judy wondered if he'd drifted off again.

"That's what I always say." Then he whispered, "Good thing he's gone. This here, this'd kill him."

While Duffy dozed beside her on the couch, Judy wept silently. It was true; Duffy had never once raised his voice to her. They'd never had a fight, not once in all their time. They never really had a reason. But sitting beside him on the couch, Judy stung with anger. She wanted to pick a fight and for him to fight back. She wanted a fight, wanted to vent her outrage over this disease, over Duffy's dying, over her having to be strong and brave and him going to leave her all alone. She wanted to fight and to make up and for the cancer to just be gone once they'd cleared the air.

She listened to his rattling breath as he slept, looked upon his face, gaunt and gray. She would not pick a fight with him now. They would both remain polite and impassive until it was over.

After Duffy died his friends allowed as how his good luck streak continued right to the very end, how he would have wanted it that way; to just keel over working on his chainsaw, to have finished the job he started. But they weren't there. He'd spared them, had them thinking he was getting well and resting up for the next adventure. Judy was there, but he'd misled her too.

That morning Duffy said he was getting dressed and going to the shed.

"Whatever for, Duffy? Don't you want to rest?"

"Ah, Judy I've been resting so much. I gotta do somethin'. I feel good today. I gotta do somethin'." Judy helped him get dressed, helped him out the door and across the yard to the shed. She helped him but believed he was stronger. She left him at his workbench.

"I wanna tune up this chainsaw. Been meanin' to do that. You go on in, Judy, I'm fine."

She did as she was asked and went back to the house. She heard the saw running a few times, knew that he was making adjustments. When she didn't hear it for a while she checked in on him. He was filing the chain and didn't notice her. She silently retreated, leaving him to his task.

When she returned a half hour later the saw was all wiped down, sitting on the bench. All the tools were put away. Duffy was sprawled on the floor, coughing violently, dark bloody bubbles clinging to his unshaven chin. Judy choked back a scream. Duffy looked at her wild-eyed, coughed again then lay still. Judy ran back to the trailer. She called 911 because she didn't know what else to do. Duffy's luck had run out.

Worry about her own luck stole in furtively with the silence that followed in the cold and dusty wake of the sirens.

COLD (1)

It was cold outside. He was tired of being cold, cold and hungry. He knew how to get three squares, a warm bed. This time he'd make sure he was set for life.

The last thing the old woman saw was prison-inked knuckles desperately gripping a knife.

THE BUS STOP

The fat man isn't waiting for the bus. You see him walking down the sidewalk as the bus pulls over to a stop. Green polyester pants are tucked into unbuckled snowmobile boots and a wool checkered shirt is buttoned all the way up, even the collar, tight around his neck. His wet mouth is open as he walks looking straight ahead, lurching slightly with each step. You watch safely from the bus window. He doesn't seem to even notice the bus, then just steps on, the doors thudding shut behind him. You feel sorry for the girl he drops heavily beside but are relieved that it's not you.

As the bus labors away from the curb the man mutters to himself. You study the gray tracked snow of the passing sidewalks. Everyone is working hard at ignoring the big man's awkward laughter. Everyone avoids looking at him and at the girl who is leaning toward the window, staring into a book that she has pulled from her bag.

You brave a sidelong glance as he speaks to the girl, as she politely but tersely confirms that she is a student at the university. Between his high-pitched, panting giggle and thrusting small talk at the girl he whispers cannily to himself. The girl clings to her book, holding it like a shield in front of her.

The fat man breaks off his whispering and demands to know of the girl why she reads so much. He smells, even from your seat you can smell him. His face is craggy and purple blotched. A spot of something neglected in the bristle of his chin glistens. When the girl doesn't answer right away he asks his question again in a slightly higher pitch. She makes an answer while trying not to smell him or see him or touch him.

She gathers up her bag, stuffing the book in as the bus pulls over to another stop. She squeezes by him and hops down the steps of the rear door. She walks briskly away, her chin tucked down into her collar, hands deep in her coat pockets. The fat man makes a shadow as he stands up. You hear him giggling and whispering as he lumbers off the bus. He lurches calmly after the girl, big chapped hands at his sides. The bus pulls away.

SPINNING

Legends persisted, though raggedly recalled, of a malevolent spirit that lingers about the lake. They sat up late speculating on the tale, spinning stories of hauntings, spooking one another at the fringe of the campfire's dancing glow.

Paddling out on the sun sparkled water the next day, they eagerly explored each cove of the tree-lined lake, their nighttime entertainment forgotten.

Floating on a glassy line of symmetry, paddles at rest across the coamings of their kayaks, they marveled at the reflections on the surface. They peered into the depths to see the inversion, treetops wavering in the blue sky in the water beneath them.

A sense of disembodiment came with the realization that they themselves showed no reflection, nor a shadow. Fear caught them in a current of watery treetops. They drifted down, down, higher and higher into a bottomless liquid sky.

THE WELL

They were very pleased with the place, such a deal, all they had wished for, despite its rundown condition, the lack of power and water. For now they had toted drinking water in, with a plan to maybe later dig out the old well.

They went down to the well and dropped a rock, then another and another, listening for its landing in the dark below, hoping for a splash, but hearing nothing at all, not even the tunk of rock on dirt.

But later, when she returned to the well for her forgotten sunglasses, she thought she heard a gurgling sound. Another dropped stone sounded a very clear splash, though very far down. The next day the water level was visible. They rigged a rope and bucket and drew water. Later they would have it tested for potability but for this trip they were motivated to start cleaning the long unused cabin.

That night she remarked how strange the change in water level seemed, but he tiredly mumbled reassuring words about water tables and springs and how they simply didn't hear the splash at first. They both were soon asleep after a good day's work.

They woke at dawn's light, which shimmered on the water that now lapped over the top step and under the door of the cabin on the little rise of land overlooking the engulfed well.

***

Rushing from their beds to the front porch, standing in water up over their knees, they were shaken not just by the unfathomable water, but by silence; the absence of birdsong, of rustling grasses and leaves, of any sound, save themselves. Except for the steady rise of water, all was still; even the spread of dawn's light seemed to have stopped, arrested low on the tree-topped horizon.

"How can this be?" he queried, scanning in vain for the car, though it clearly would offer no escape.

They looked at each other with a hope of relief when the water, up to their waists now as they clung to the porch posts, ceased rising. Then they felt a shaking, a tremor. The water pulled at them in a rushing tide, sweeping them off the porch and swirling helplessly in a whirlpool that drained into the old well, now visible in the wet and matted yard. At the end of the rutted lane, beyond the dripping car, the for-sale sign that they had neglected to remove listed in the sodden ground.

HARVEST TOURS

"At Harvest Farms we recycle, reuse, and compost year-round."

He appraised the gaits of the elderly tour group as they went ahead into the facility. There were sure to be titanium joints, probably pacemakers, definitely hearing aids. The door closed.

The next tour, a busload of young recidivists, would be harder. It always was but even without the hardware it's where the profits were. Their organs and tissues brought twice the price as those of these old people.

After work he drank heavily, with full knowledge that he was devaluing his own liver.

SPACES

Increasingly, ordinary situations brought on the terror. Being in a car was intolerable; worse was enduring the press of public transportation. People. Any gathering of people became unbearable, even one or two friends an encroachment. She needed space.

Inside spaces needed to be tidy and organized, ruthlessly uncluttered. She spent more time out of doors, walked often and far, but even there began to feel hemmed in not just by other walkers and narrow paths, but even by trees and hills, hovering encircling topographies.

She moved to North Dakota, into an old farmhouse with a big open porch overlooking miles and miles of flat prairie, surrounded by a vast expanse of wheat fields. She came to feel enclosed by this surrounding of wheat that whispered and swayed in the wind, so was grateful for the combines that came and left behind only silent stubble. This was soon covered by snow.

Cold drove her indoors. Alone and with no escape, would she again feel crowded, jostled and shoved by the doubts and fears that trolled her imagination, or would she find expansion there in her solitude?

Blowing snow drifted onto the porch behind her, swept through the door left open to the prairie blizzard. She disappeared into the unbroken endless white.

SLIP

Still in her nightclothes, she stands in the damp grass watching the swirling morning fog that veils the lake, strands of wispy gray unwinding skyward, wraithlike, the mist thick enough to conceal the loons that call mournfully. Their molting is almost complete, signaling their departure, signaling ice up, winter. She envies the loons' ability to molt and migrate. Turning over the old canoe, she leaves her nightclothes at the water's edge, floats paddle-less, the slight breeze whispering her into the fog. The water is warmer than the cool air that eddies around her. With barely a splash she lets herself slip into its consoling embrace.

ASHES, ASHES

She lit the burner, set the pages in the flames. She would silence the voices, the quiet ones as well as the loud ones. She stumbled to the couch, trusting the fire to consume what she had fed it.

Fire, though, it might start on one thing, nibble, and then gulp greedily before moving on, leaving untouched crumbs behind.

The firemen would discover her lifeless form on the couch; in the kitchen a melted pill bottle; enough charred remnants of writing that her small voice could yet be heard.

ECHOES

Jagged edged echoes rip the night quiet apart. She struggles in silence to keep from drowning in the din. Epicenter of awful knowing, she lays quiet and still as red and blue lights claw at the windows, shred the darkness, send shadows reeling like banshees about the house. She remains frozen, unwilling, unable, to face what they will find. This time they will not come in to see her, always ready to forgive, holding her son, pleading with him. It's over. He has ended his addiction. This time their Narcan won't bring him back.

SPRING CLEANING

Their marriage lasted longer than most of their long-time friends', who often remarked how wonderful that they never argued.

It was true, they didn't. "Life's too short to argue," he'd always said. "Marriage is about compromise." She remembered his words like it was only yesterday. In fact it was only yesterday, spring-cleaning day. He was a good sport to help with the cleaning.

"It's my retirement too," she had said, steadying the ladder as he wiped down the ceiling fan. He didn't want to argue; he didn't want to compromise either.

All their friends would know that his death was accidental.

COLD (2)

Problems get worked out in the woodshed. Punishments get meted there. Sometimes both.

A thick trickle like ink from his silent mouth tells his final tale, the scene held fast by the cold. She leaves quickly, no cordwood in her arms.

TIDINGS

Usually he sleeps through her early morning swim, at most is pouring coffee as she flip-flops out the door, towel over her shoulder. Today they both rise early. Today he watches her disappear down the beach path.

Today, her flip-flops and towel left behind, she walks where waves erase her footsteps, stops finally to face the dawn-jeweled ocean. She draws a deep breath sweet with the scent of beach roses before plunging in.

Today she floats, lets the rip current carry her out beyond the breakers, far from shore. Today she won't make the doctor's appointment.

THE CARDIGAN

From the school bus a cat can be seen at the edge of the gravel road, a white cat that slips through the roadside weeds then saunters along the brook back towards the schoolhouse. Who knows whose cat? Just something seen from the bus, still within sight of the school.

The next day a white cat is at the front of the school when the bus pulls to a stop at the doors. From the bus it is seen carefully edging along the basement windows set in the school's brick foundation. The cat is unusual not just for being at school, and not just for its entirely white fur, but most remarkably for its eyes. For just a moment it looks in the direction of the bus, and its eyes are seen to be of two different colors, one green and one amber. The bus empties, students filing down the treaded step and into the double doors of the school. The sun, now brushing the dusty high windows of the fourth grade classroom, has warmed the last of the night's frost from the grass, from the bushes below by the brook. The cat is gone from sight as the students stumble and scramble from bus to building.

In the wide, open hallway that is central to the four classrooms of the old building a new student is spotted. No one at this school dresses like this girl; no one wears a clean white button up sweater or white leotards with a pleated skirt. This girl was not on the bus; she must have walked with the village kids. She looks slight, could be a fourth grader but she does not go into that classroom. She must be in fifth grade. There are no words in the hall, just a glance and wondering at the sight of an unfamiliar student, a quiet blonde girl in a white cardigan sweater.

At recess the girl is alone. There is a silence that surrounds her, that shrouds her from the other children whose boisterous noise of play bubbles and roils from across the yard where they swing and slide and jump rope, oblivious to the new girl who lingers in the shadow of the school building, edges along the basement wall, traces the bricks with a lazy finger. When approached she looks up. The cardigan, so white, and the very fine, very light blond hair, and the cheeks with a hint of pink, those are not the most striking aspect of this quiet girl. It is her eyes, one green and the other amber. She pauses, almost as if she will turn and run, but then she smiles slightly, continues to silently slink along the side of the school. There is respectful imitation and cautious, wordless questioning, two girls lingering in the quiet beside the building, tracing the bricks, then one again as the third and fourth graders get called in ahead of the older students. A hasty glance from this bustling line reveals a glimpse of white as the new girl rounds the corner of the building, sliding out of sight. Swept along, filing into the building, the normal noise of the rest of the children returns to focus. The day ticks on until the bus returns.

In the rush to the bus and a window seat, the new girl is not seen in the hallway, not spied through the open door of the fifth grade classroom. From the bus a cat is seen, a white cat with one green eye and one amber. It slips around the far side of the building, from the playground side, and sits on its haunches on the packed gravel by the brick foundation. It shows a pink pad and pink nose as it delicately wipes at its face. The cat looks up as the hinged door is pulled closed. Then it disappears into the bushes beyond the flagpole, the bushes that shield the brook that runs through the village. The bus grinds away.

The next day, eagerly anticipated, bears disappointment. There is no cat. There is no new girl; nor the next day, nor the next. It's as if there never was.

SMALL WORLD PLAY

"Still at it, are you, crafting your little fairy houses?"

She smiled indulgently at her neighbor. *Poor thing, how many times do I need to explain that the fairy houses and other constructions are for when my granddaughters come to visit, that the girls delight in small-world play?*

"Still, I must say, it's very clever, what you create with scrap wood, sticks, and a hot-glue gun, very clever."

Must you say it? You say it every time you come by, poor daffy thing. And it isn't meant to be clever or crafty, it's just something to encourage magical small-world play for the darling granddaughters, while they are still of an age for that kind of thing.

Though she had to admit to taking pleasure in the making of the miniatures, anticipating as she worked the child-wisdom that would inform their play. She looked forward to listening in to their invocations when they discovered the addition of the little wooden cross on the top of the main house.

The neighbor let herself out, shaking her head. She remembered what the older woman wouldn't. She remembered that horrible night many years ago; the accident that claimed the only daughter along with her two little girls.

SQUALL LINE

She battens the hatches, would weather another one out; these storms never last more than three days.

They always manage to arrive within moments of each other.

Three cars' worth of doors fling open at once, spill grandchildren who swirl behind their parents, the mass of them a squall line bearing down, gusting through the front door without so much as a knock, her daughters' smiles flashing like lightning.

The men and children retreat to the beach while the daughters assault her home; dusting; scrubbing; organizing her cupboards.

Erosion the aftermath; she's losing ground.

UNINITIATED

The children and grandchildren bring their signature dishes to family gatherings, but her mother remains the pie maker, piecrusts legendary, the recipe and technique a mystery. To learn it she would have to apprentice under her mother, observe and practice. That takes time. She would become initiated later.

At the last gathering even the uninitiated recognized that the slits in the top crust, usually cut so artistically, had been forgotten, the pies uncharacteristically soggy.

At this gathering they mine their pie with worried forks, something less obvious forgotten.

She would never learn the mystery.

IDLING

Fingers cracking the pod and rolling the peas out into the pot in one deft move. Had that favorite paring knife, remember, always got the thinnest peel off a potato, all in one piece. She taught us to knit though none of us could ever get our needles clacking as fast as hers. She even tickled trout, would go down to the brook and get all she wanted with not a line or a net.

Now she lies in bed, papery hands fluttering to her face over and over, like she can't believe she's still here.

THE MUSEUM

"'Caution, Entrance Only'. Guess if it's 'entrance only' I don't have to worry too much about getting run down by people exiting." He chuckled at the sign that he read out loud to himself, continued down the tree shaded lane to the *Museum of Memories and Moments,* already pleased with his decision to check out this quirky sounding private museum found off the beaten track, even more pleased when he noted that many of the cars in the grassed parking lot were potential museum pieces themselves, some dating back many decades.

Taking roads less traveled and making impulsive stops at unusual sites was the theme of his meandering road trip across the country, begun soon after his wife finally died, which, he would agree, doesn't sound so good in the telling, unless one knew that she had suffered from Alzheimer's, that he had mourned her passing years ago even as he stuck by her side, learning to do for himself as he learned to do for her.

Now he was on an extended vacation, the type of unfocused and unplanned trip that his wife never would have enjoyed but that gave him the time and space he needed before facing the empty house and a life without her, unencumbered now, but truly alone.

Seeing not one other person, not even the proprietor, he surmised that it was an honor system, expected to pay upon exiting, cash stuffed into a lock box. He took his time wandering in and out of old buildings, intrigued by eclectic displays and intricate models, musing whether it was the collection or the collector being presented. He continued in this manner until he was stopped cold by a diorama.

In perfect scale and detail were the museum and its buildings as well as the parking lot with the antique and vintage cars he had seen earlier. But the dusty diorama also included his late model car, parked less than two hours previous. Heart racing, he hurried back to the parking lot, past his car to the lot's edge until he was stopped, the 'Caution, Entrance Only' sign visible through the glass wall that contained him.

He walked back to the museum grounds, knowing that he'd find his house but unsure what would be on exhibit. He hoped that he might find her there, her before the illness.

COLD (3)

Phone and electric out. She gave him aspirin, stoked the fire, bundled up. Stumbled through the snow towards the neighbors, praying he'd hang on.

Arriving on snow-machines to check in, they found him weak but fine.

Outside the wind blew, temperatures dropping.

Where was his wife?

TIME OF MONSTERS

It was a great year; at least it seemed that way at first. Books about Bigfoot and the Loch Ness monster and the Bermuda Triangle were read and reread and passed around. When they showed the movie about Bigfoot sightings in the district high school auditorium we all went. The debates about real or fake were frequent, believers versus non-believers. Sometimes there were well-reasoned arguments; some arguments were just dumb. The most hotly debated topic though was wrestling, probably because it was on TV almost every Saturday night. It's not like we had a lot of channels, only one, sometimes two, so we all watched Saturday Night Wrestling. No one could believe it when Saturday Night Wrestling came to town. Everyone went to see it in the high school gym.

Everyone was there, so yeah, she was there, probably. It sure seemed like all the sixth graders were there and some younger kids, little brothers and sisters, some older kids too. The high school gym was packed; kids from all the surrounding towns went to see the Saturday Night Wrestlers.

Yeah, even if you weren't a fan of wrestling, even if you didn't believe it was real. Because isn't that why you watch it on TV, to critique it and look for the obvious fake moves, the rehearsed stunts? And then it was here, all those famous Saturday Night Wrestling guys were here, live. We went to see it for ourselves, to settle the real versus fake question once and for all. Some people went just to see real stars from TV. I mean how often do you get to see someone that only exists on TV? This wasn't the grainy black and white and gray images from TV. This was in color. Real. Live. We could see the sweat glistening on the wrestlers, grimaced in disgust when the sweat flew from their bodies and onto the older kids sitting in the folding chair seats near the ring. The bleachers were better seats.

So yeah, everyone was in the bleachers, everyone in fifth, sixth grade. She could have been, maybe even with her younger sister. A lot of us got stuck with our younger sisters or brothers. This was a drop-off event, a stream of station wagons and pickup trucks disgorging excited kids at the side entrance to the gym to enter there and see it transformed into a scene from television, with only the ring in the center lit up. There was just enough light at the edges to spot friends and climb the bleachers to sit with them and chew gum and point out all the wrestlers that we recognized from Saturday Night Wrestling. It was a great night. Mighty Marceau the giant Frenchman was there! I said he looked even bigger in real-life; others said he looked smaller. In one match Mighty Marceau somehow got all twisted up in the ropes then twanged loudly onto the floor. Then, big as he is, he leapt back into the ring, light as a cat, holding a metal folding chair in his hands. Wham! He brought it right down on Dangerous Dan's head. Dangerous Dan swayed, his head twirling before he whomped onto the mat. It was like a cartoon. I said it was too much like a cartoon, but others insisted that's what it looks like, that's what it sounds like, that is what it's like when a giant slams a chair down on someone's head. The fake versus real debate was not settled.

No, I don't remember actually seeing her. I sat with my friends. She could have been there though. She's the kind of person you don't really notice. She wouldn't have joined a group or anything. A long time ago we used to invite her to sleepovers but she never came, her father never let her. The grownups always only said her father is very protective of her since her mother died. I don't ever remember her having a mother. I hardly saw her father, just sometimes when he'd pick her up at school in their old Ford. That night a lot of the grownups were playing cards at someone's house in the village while they waited for us rather than go all the way home. But he wouldn't have been with them. I never saw her father with the other grownups.

I don't know, maybe she wasn't there. She never talked on the bus about wrestling, or Bigfoot, or anything, but I think she listened in. I know once on the bus she did talk to me about TV. She said then that sometimes she was able to stay up as late as she wanted and on those nights she would watch TV until when the Star Spangled Banner came on before they went off the air. Then she would finally turn the TV off and would watch the square of light grow smaller and smaller until it finally blinked out and the screen was dark, but somehow still glowing in the late night. She lit up as she talked about watching television in the dark of night. She was a little strange but I wish she'd talked more. I wish she'd sometimes joined the rest of us. I guess it's too late now.

That night was something. There was always a show in and around the ring. Even when the wrestlers were in their corners another one would be doing something sneaky, even whalloping the announcer and even the referee once. Then there was a big ruckus as that wrestler had to be subdued and removed from the ring and then the referee and the announcer got into it with each other. It was quite a show. All eyes were on that ring. But at one point I did look away and at just that time one of the wrestlers was crossing through the forgotten dim past the ring, across the gym, making his way to the locker room. The light was just enough to see that his tights were shabby and dirty, that he was tired, even sad maybe. It was like seeing forgotten balloons days after the party, faded and losing air, that wrestler leaving the lit up ring. I followed with my eyes as he went through the door and down the hall, and beyond that I saw the old paint-flaked bus parked outside. The wrestlers must all have come in on that bus together and would all leave on it together, all their enmity dropped like a used towel at the edge of the wrestling ring. What I chanced to see was real. I never said anything about that tired old wrestler, but I did not get into the debates on the school bus after that either. The stuff that went on in the ring was fake but the wrestlers were real.

Of course I don't believe that one of the wrestlers took her or that she got on their bus that night. They say that her father believes that. Say he says those Saturday Night Wrestling guys took her or that she ran off that night. The sheriff, whose main job is taking beer away from the high school boys, says 'girls will be girls'. He says that there's no evidence of wrongdoing so he is doing nothing about it. The sheriff says that the case remains open, but it's too late to question anyone because the wrestlers have returned to TV where they belong. He says he will keep a close eye on them there.

So now, she who was almost invisible is famous for having disappeared. Some of the kids say that she was there that night but walked home and got kidnapped by a Bigfoot. Or she was never there that night and Bigfoot took her right out of her trailer. A few kids have hypothesized about a Bermuda Triangle in the area and they say to be very careful, hers won't be the last mysterious disappearance. Most say that she did end up with the Saturday Night Wrestling guys, that she went there that night and climbed onto their old Greyhound during the show. They even say to just watch, watch Saturday Night Wrestling real careful and you'll see her on the TV, hiding from Dangerous Dan behind Mighty Marceau.

I don't watch wrestling on TV much anymore. I know they are just real now, the wrestlers. I also know that they didn't do anything. They didn't take her; they didn't take anything when they came to town. But for some reason I feel scared, more scared than from any Bigfoot movie or monster book I ever read, a quiet pit of the stomach scared. Because it wasn't the wrestlers and it wasn't Bigfoot or any triangle. I wonder if the sheriff ever bothered to ask the sister about that night. That's who you should ask, the little sister.

The sister is small, quiet and withdrawn, slipping on and off the bus and in and out of the school silent as a ghost. One day I finally spoke to the little sister because I just felt so weird about what happened. I didn't know what to say really, I don't know what I did say, but I learned that the little sister likes to watch TV, but never wrestling or any scary show. She likes the Waltons, any show with families and happy endings. She likes the TV for its light, and looks over her shoulder while watching it in the dark of her own home, ever fearful of monsters, unable to speak of what is real and what is fake.

DEEP SLEEP

The stone dreamt of cold grinding ice and was not afraid

dreamt of twisting transforming heat and was not afraid

dreamt of the crushing weight of oceans and was not afraid

dreamt of the acidic embrace of mosses and was not afraid.

The stone dreamt

of timelessness

of fearlessness.

The sleeping stone

was the Earth

was the universe

was a tossed pebble.

She awakened suddenly, slowly; acclimated to her limbs, her body.

She returned from dreams of being stone.

THE QUILL'S MAGIC
JOURNEYING

For seven days, or maybe it was seven years, or even seven lifetimes, the girl and the former soldier journeyed. They started down a well-worn path through sun-dappled woods. When a gust of wind blew the white feather from the girl's hand it drifted away into the darker woods. Without hesitation they followed to retrieve the feather though they went far and farther off the path, deep and deeper into the woods. They found the feather and found themselves they knew not where, knew only that they journeyed.

Always the girl held the white feather close. Always at night, by firelight or moonlight or starlight, the girl wrote their story with the quill. There was no shortage of ink for always there was some blood from their trials; always a tear could be wrought from their travails. Trekking across barren plains they were wind-whipped and sandblasted. They climbed jagged mountains of sharp cold stone that tore at their feet and hands as they crawled their craggy paths. They traversed a swamp that sucked at their feet, pulled at them, threatening to mire them forever. One day they found themselves in a wood so thick with thorny brush and branches they feared they could not go on.

"I wish I had my trusty sword," the soldier lamented. As soon as he had wished it, the sword was in his hands. He smiled broadly. Now he knew what to do, now he would get them out of this entanglement. Boldly he slashed and fiercely he sliced at the branches but every time he cut one it grew back three-fold, the branches becoming ever thicker. Finally the girl cried for him to stop.

"Let me try," she said, holding forth the white feather. She held it up and laid it against a branch. The branch was swept away. Again and again, one branch at a time she wielded her feather quill until finally they emerged into a clearing at the foot of a steep hill. They crawled into a cave and fell in exhaustion. Clutching the feather, clutching each other, they slept. They slept without stirring for three days, or three years, or perhaps even three lifetimes, until finally dawns' light and birds' songs drew them out.

Blinking in the light the soldier exclaimed when he looked upon the girl. "Why, you have transformed again!"

"What?" laughed the girl. "Am I a bird again?"

"No, you're a wise old woman. I mean you are a beautiful young woman. I mean... you're..."

"She is all of these. She has always been these and more."

"The bird!" Both the girl and the young man turned. There was the great bird that she had freed.

"So surprised?" said the bird. "I see that you still hold the feather. I see that it is stained and worn; well used."

The girl looked at the feather quill that she yet held in her hand even after their long time in the cave. Gently the great bird took it from her and tossed it into the air. Then all her words that she had written with the quill began to flutter and flit like damselflies, then gathered and grew into feathers to finally swirl into a flock of colorful birds that darted into the trees singing and chirping.

"These magical birds will take you wherever you wish to go. They will lift you up. You will soar with them."

The girl and the former soldier looked up to where the birds gathered, saw them whirl into winged motion, followed them as they flew into a bright blue sky.

FULL MOON TIDE

Crickets and breezy leaves lulled them as they moonbathed in the golden light that lapped the shores of their backyard. Flowing through the tree canopy, moonlight shimmered on their skin like water. As the moon rose higher another wave of light washed over them, pooling then receding, rendering them breathless. They gasped as the moonlight again rushed and curled around them, swept them up. Tumbling and rolling in the powerful swirling current, they careened over the trees, were hurtled across the sky, drawn inexorably towards the moon. Far below, Earth's oceans sparkled.

ALCHEMY

It was just an old skidder wheel-rim, but he knew he'd found gold.

"Whatever for?" she asked.

"For you," he said. "I got you a ring."

He set it in the clearing behind the house. He gathered wood. He brought seats. Friends and family often ended up there, speaking easily around the crackling fire into the night, gazing into the flames in communion, staring in silent reveries.

In daytime, empty and cool, it looked like what it was, an old rusty rim. But it was gold. She loved her fire ring.

PASSING

As the collection plate passed from pew to pew the minister intoned 'tis more blessed to give than to receive'. Some checks were placed face up and unfolded, for all to see the largesse, though most checks and cash were discreetly folded, more modestly placed. The plate clinked with unclutched coins from children who were rewarded with approving nods and smiles from their parents and the parishioners. This was a time in the service when a certain amount of surreptitious stretching and surmising happened, necks turning, eyes following the plate as it filled up, moving hand to hand then to the pew behind.

So the pause was noticeable when a slight, scruffy person, sitting at the end of a pew, head bowed, did not look up, did not deposit an offering, did not take the plate that was held out to him. After an awkward moment the plate was handed to the person in the pew behind the stranger, whose fervent focus was disconcerting to a congregation that did not recognize him.

Later some would remark on the play of light as the collection plate passed behind the stranger, how the refracted sunlight that glanced off the plate shone over his bowed head, illuminating him, appearing for all the world like a halo.

SHOWING UP

"I can't arrest someone if there is no crime, you know that, Reverend, and I can't see as how this stranger has committed a crime, can you?"

"It's vagrancy! This stranger keeps showing up around town and where is he sleeping at night, huh? Where is he at night, whose backyard is he in?"

"Reverend, is he still attending your church services?"

"Yes, he is, and I have to tell you it has been quite distracting, what with everyone gaping at this guy all through my sermons. Many have even started imitating him, just praying away, oblivious to the proceedings."

The sheriff's brows went up. With a slight bemused smile he asked if the reverend wanted him to string the stranger up.

"Of course not, Thomas, come on. But you know bums like him are always bad for business. You have to run him out of town."

"Sure thing, Reverend. If he crosses my path, I'll nail him for you."

"Okay, laugh now, Thomas. Don't say I didn't warn you."

"See you in church, Reverend."

AGAPE

Hanging up his coat and hat, the Reverend affixed a smile when he heard Mary speaking with someone in the dining room but that smile quickly folded in surprise when he recognized the stranger from his church seated at the head of the table, set for three.

"Welcome home, Dear. I want you to meet Josiah, whom I have invited to have dinner with us- and to stay in the guest room for a while."

The reverend's mouth was agape as the stranger spoke, his eyes shining warmly. "It is true Christian spirit, Reverend, to break bread with me and to offer a bed to me, a poor traveling preacher."

Before the Reverend could respond, his wife cheerfully reported that Josiah was willing to lead the congregation while they went on a long overdue vacation, and wasn't this a godsend, she marveled, a traveling preacher?

The Reverend swallowed the rest of the wine from his wife's cup before sitting heavily in an uncustomary seat beside her at the table. The traveling preacher planned aloud his first sermon, to be based, he said, on a quote he attributed to Jimi Hendrix; 'When the power of love overcomes the love of power, the world will know peace'.

SINGING THEIR JOY

The People hear their clan singing their joy at returning, their chirps and squeals, their clicking talk. We gather to greet them, also singing happiness, laughing and talking as we keep watch. We can see their spiraled tusks, but these ones are too far off, these ones are not ready.

Hundreds more are returning to us. For both clans it is a time of feasting. There will be those who will come close, will give themselves to the People. We are grateful, waste nothing. We carve their stories in ivory, that the tuugaalik will live forever.

RIPPED

Just one of the guys at the shop, Marge was a hell of a woman. Marge did as much or more work and heavy lifting than the guys she worked with; she also ate as much, or more, and drank as much, or more. Confident and capable, Marge liked to claim that she put her big-girl panties on one leg at a time, just like the rest and the best of them.

It was a good thing, this matter of wearing big girl panties, for it was they that showed prominently after a bend-over for a dropped wrench rent wide her oil stained Dickies. The guys cracked smiles at 'the rip heard round the shop'. They joked, noting that Marge had indeed gotten too big for her britches.

TOE TO TOE

"Excuse me boys," Marge said, abruptly putting her beer down. "But I spy a man." Marge Small felt something she'd not felt before, at least not as she could remember. Marge was smitten. Ignoring the raised eyebrows of her drinking companions, the guys from the shop, Marge headed straight across the barroom to where Ernest Biggs sat alone at the corner table watching the band.

The first thing that Marge had noticed was his boots, boots just like hers, leather work boots with scuffed steel toes. The second and more compelling thing that Marge noticed were his hands, large even on his large frame, seeming almost a nuisance to the knobby wrists they hung from, almost a threat to the mug of beer they dwarfed. She immediately got to imagining how a hand like that on the small of her back would make the small of her back feel... *small*. By the time Marge arrived at Ernest Bigg's table she was all swelled up inside with feeling dainty and delicate and smitten. She sat down across from Ernest.

In his lifetime Ernest had rarely- no, never- been approached by a woman of any sort for any reason. In a slow series of bumbling, fumbling movements Ernest quickly stood up. Then, mumbling a red-faced introduction, he promptly sat back down. Marge stood up.

"Come on," she told the big, bewildered man. "Let's dance."

Marge Small grasped one of those big hands and Ernest Biggs was dragged to the dance floor, stumbling helplessly, much to the amusement of Marge's coworkers, who watched from their perches at the bar. The guys from the shop had no doubt who would lead in this dance.

The guys watched as if viewing a sporting event. Bets were made. They watched and commented as how it wasn't a pretty thing they watched, this four-handed creature with at least three left feet lurching all over the dance floor. It took a couple innings for them to realize that their pal Marge was deaf and indifferent to their remarks, that she was not coming back even for her unfinished beer. A bit disoriented without Marge to call for shots, the guys trickled out, missing the overtime inning when they would have seen Ernest Biggs finally finding his balance even if it meant holding on to Marge, his large palms gentle on her hips, on the small of her back during a slow dance; when they would have seen Marge with bent head resting on Ernest's chest, smiling down at scuffed work boots going toe to toe; would have seen Ernest beginning to lead, Marge beginning to yield.

Finally, wearing shy smiles, Marge and Ernest went back to the corner table.

"This is new territory for me," Marge said.

"Oh, not me, I come here a lot to hear the music, that is I used to. This is my first time back since …"

"No, I was speaking metaphorically," Marge interrupted. "I don't usually do…"

"Oh, yeah, right… Me either."

"I like your boots."

"Thanks, I like yours too."

"Yeah, they're comfortable and sturdy."

"Me too. I mean mine too. My boots."

"What work do you do in your work boots, Ernest?"

"I'm a mechanic."

"Me too!"

"Got my own little place."

"Work for yourself?"

"Yeah, by myself. I mean for myself."

"Nice setup?"

"Yeah, two bays, two lifts."

"Plenty of business?"

"Yeah... Marge?"

"Yes, Ernest?"

"I could use another man."

The guys at her old shop told Marge-stories long after she had gone, long after she left to swing her wrenches alongside Ernest Biggs.

TRAILING

The trail started with boots, the boots preceding pants. Sharp eyes might notice that the smaller pair of work pants on the floor had been mended. Those same eyes will follow the trail to its conclusion, a bed somewhat stressed by the additional weight it carried into the morning, the morning Ernest Biggs did not wake up alone, a situation that brought him some happy anxiousness.

Shyly, cautiously, he rolled over towards his bedmate, ripping a fart as he did so. He reddened, but her laughter and admirable retort put him at ease.

"I always return fire," she said.

"Mornin', Marge."

DRESSING

Hugh Heffner always had a robe, Ernest realized, but all he had was not-so-whitey-not-so-tighties, and those not within reach.

There were many reasons why the undressing was not strongly imprinted on the template of Ernest's memory. Beer, darkness, and excitement had all conspired to make the undressing a manageable if not memorable experience but now Ernest felt trapped in his own bed. Marge was still at his side, and he was uncertain when it might be okay to recover his clothes, was now uncomfortable at the prospect of being out of them in front of her. He retreated under the covers.

But then Marge just rolled out on the other side of the bed and without a stitch started backtracking, picking up shirts and pants and even boots, gathering up each piece of their clothing until she stood beside the bed, stood before Ernest holding their clothes, outer and under together, and asked if he supposed it was time to get dressed, maybe go pick up her Craftsman rolling tool chest now.

New as he was to having a woman in his life, Ernest recognized that through her initiative with the clothes gathering Marge was telling him- with her question she was in fact *telling* him that it was time to get dressed and go get her tools.

And Ernest, new as he was to all of this and in spite of the fact that he knew what she expected him to say, he looked at this naked woman holding his clothes with her clothes and he said no, it wasn't time, her Craftsman rolling tool chest could wait, that getting dressed might take a while.

STUMPED

Outside the department store fitting-room, balanced like a crane, left pant leg dragging dangerously near her one right foot, Ilene Higginbottom was hopping mad, squawking loudly that she'd lost her leg.

"Oh, yes," said Ernest, trying to help, "I heard, the accident at the mill…"

"No, I've lost my prosthetic leg. It's disappeared while I was trying on pants. I set it down and now I can't find it."

Just then an apologetic sales clerk appeared and presented the leg to Ilene Higginbottom, explaining that she had taken it from the fitting room thinking it was meant for a stocking display.

Ernest shared the story with Marge that evening. "You met Ilene Higginbottom, the woman who is suing the mill where she worked for the loss of her leg? I've been following that case. You know, if it goes to court she may not have a leg to stand on."

SPRING AND EVERYTHING

"Why were you at the department store, anyway?"

Ernest handed Marge a large box.

"It's so light."

Marge lifted the lid off the box. Three red balloons floated out.

"Three months together, a whole season. Winter to spring."

"Honestly, Ernest, how sweet."

"Box ain't empty yet, Marge."

"Well! This ain't yer mother's overalls!"

Turning as red as the tethered helium balloons that squeaked against each other on the ceiling, Ernest explained that the large slinky garment was called a teddy.

Marge led the way, Ernest bumping behind her, balloons bumping behind him, and yes, he had some other latex. He'd thought of everything.

STRAWBERRY MOON

Marge sat at the table poring over a seed catalog, one of the balloons a strawberry moon overhead.

"I want carrot cake Ernest, that's what."

"There's some at the store."

"I want to make it."

"We can buy carrots."

"No, I wanna grow the carrots."

"Well gee Marge, it's gonna take a long while to get that cake."

"Yes, well into summer."

"Why wait so long? Why work so hard?"

"It's to celebrate. Us. You like balloons, I like cake."

Ernest grinned. Marge would be baking. Here, come summer.

"I'll dig the garden patch, Marge."

"That's what I figured."

DOUBLE WIDE

Working together inside his two-bay garage, Ernest and Marge were a well-oiled machine, professional and productive, she following his lead with the respect that she always showed a boss, the owner of the shop. After work Marge usually went with Ernest to the humble trailer he called home, just behind the shop. It was there that he didn't know what to expect, like her going right to the bedroom and emptying his drawers.

"Ernest, you only wear the same few things as long as I've known you. What are all these clothes, taking up space?"

"Those are the ones I used to wear, but they, uh, well they don't fit anymore."

"Well they don't fit in your bureau, neither. We gotta make room if I'm gonna double the population of your singlewide. So here, I'll keep these shirts here and make curtains for the windows with them, I can't believe you don't have curtains. You take the rest of these to use as rags in the shop, we need rags in the shop, Ernest, and there, now I have some room for my clothes. Because how can I be expected to make a carrot cake this summer if I'm not right here to tend the garden and to get to know the oven."

Ernest Biggs, blushing and smiling incredulously, was thus informed by Marge Small that she would be moving in with him permanently.

"Gosh, Marge, I thought you'd never ask."

FULL HOUSE FLUSH

Ernest was to find out a few things after Marge moved in. He found out that Wednesday was poker night and that his trailer home was the new favored location for the game. The guys from Marge's old shop came by, sat on their coolers of beer around the coffee table, Marge dealing nachos and bean dip along with her colorful remarks. Ernest also found out, that first time, that not only he was not very good at poker, he also did not care for the loud bantering of the group.

So the next Wednesday Ernest declared it his pub night, and he went out for the first time since meeting Marge over three months before. The table near the small corner stage was empty and he sat there by himself as he had so often used to do. This time he was not to be left alone. He was to find out that he was, for the first time ever, noticeable.

Though it was fairly busy, the waitress came right away, called him by name, welcomed him back, asked how he was, where had he been. Ernest blushed and mumbled that he'd been busy. He was glad when she left to get his beer and gladder still when she brought it to him quickly then was quickly called away.

The waitress had no sooner left when an energetic, big haired woman bee-lined for his table, leading with the drink grasped in her right hand, listing a little to the left because of her prosthetic leg. She was talking at Earnest well before she plunked herself down in the chair beside him.

"Hi. Remember me? From the department store? Ilene. Ilene Higginbottom."

Ernest stood awkwardly, bumping the table and spilling both their drinks. The waitress came by, wiped the table while winking at Ernest, promised to bring another round.

Ilene then bombarded Ernest with compliments. "You were so kind, so helpful in the department store. I said to myself, now there's a good man."

Ernest took on the color of a radish.

"So tall, so handsome."

No one had ever told Ernest that he was handsome. He squirmed uncomfortably, turned a deeper shade of radish.

The band had started playing, and Ilene Higginbottom asked Ernest if he would like to dance.

"Oh, gosh, please, no, I, uh, I'm no good, I have two left feet."

There isn't a radish that could now compare to Ernest's red face as he remembered that Ilene Higginbottom had only one right foot. He gulped and stared at his boots. Ilene Higginbottom didn't slow down a bit.

"Ah, poor thing, I was joking, you dear, sweet man... You know, I settled out of court with the mill. I am pretty comfortable, if you know what I mean."

Ernest wasn't exactly sure what she meant. He did know that he was incredibly uncomfortable, especially when Ilene Higginbotttom leaned in and stroked his big calloused hand. He took a deep breath and stood up carefully, not spilling a thing. Ernest would never have the vocabulary to describe the range of emotions that he felt at being able to honestly tell Ilene Higginbottom that he was taken by another. But he did tell her, with relief and with pride, and then asked her to please excuse him, that he was late for his poker game.

Without even having finished a beer, Ernest left the pub, feeling kind of attractive. He was willing to bet that Marge would think so too.

LINES CAST

"Ernest, let's go fishing, catch some perch for our dinner."

"Oh, Marge, I don't fish. I don't have a pole or anything."

"What? Ernest, I had no idea, you poor thing. Well you can use one of mine. I'll show you all you need to know."

The second thing Ernest needed to know, according to Marge, was how to cast. She had him use a lure because the first thing he needed to know-baiting a hook- was impossibly hindered by his sausage-like digits and, he discovered, was incompatible with his delicate constitution.

Neither Marge nor Ernest wished to wet their feet in the icy cold water of early spring. With a long stick they managed to retrieve the pole that Ernest inadvertently cast into the pond. Eventually the pole remained in Ernest's hands more consistently and only the lure flew about in all directions, at times even smacking down on the water.

"Ernest, you stay here and practice your casting and reeling. I'm gonna try my luck further down."

Moving away Marge could hear the click of his bail being opened, the whip of the pole tip, the line singing out. Expecting to hear the lure hit the water, she instead felt a sting. The weight of the lure and the velocity of Ernest's cast ensured that the treble hook pierced right through her pants and had a good purchase in her ample cheek.

Later that evening Marge stood rather than sat at the counter as she and Ernest ate their fish dinner, take-out from the diner following a trip to the ER. Ernest continued to mumble apologies and concerns even though Marge was already joking about him being a pain in her ass.

Later in the week Marge caught fresh perch while Ernest watched. He was hooked on Marge but had all he needed to know about fishing.

NESTING

Seemed like every time Ernest tried to do for Marge he was done for.

"Ernest, did you notice that bird's nest in the rafters? El Camino's gettin' shit on."

"I'll move it."

"I figured."

Ernest had hoisted the ladder and climbed most of the way up when Marge told him she'd figured he'd move the El Camino, not the nest.

The mother robin became used to Ernest and Marge sitting quietly in their camp chairs in the late afternoon, enjoying their beer, watching as she sat the nest, then after the eggs hatched marveling at her deliveries of squirming meals.

They were both there when one by one the fledglings perched at the edge of the crowded nest before falling away into a first fluttery flight, landing bewildered in a nearby tree, past where the El Camino was parked uncovered, away from bird splatterings but now dull and dust pocked.

"Look Ernest, the young ones' chests are speckled, kind of like the El Camino is now." When Marge wondered aloud where she might point her camp chair now that the robin family was all done with the nest Ernest immediately retrieved the ladder, anxious to sanitize the carport and return the El Camino to its spot.

Ernest had hoisted the ladder and climbed most of the way up when Marge shared that the mama robin would likely reuse the nest for her next year's brood.

Ernest came down empty-handed and put the ladder away while Marge got them both another beer.

LAWDY MAMA

"Bring the El Camino over by the hose, Ernest, and I'll help you wash it. We'll get her all shiny and ship shape again, get her ready for sale."

Ernest opened the driver's side door, carefully lowered and levered himself into the seat, the fuzzy dice swaying and swinging from the rearview as the El Camino rocked with his effort. Three turns of the key got the motor running; the Steppenwolf tape that was in the dashboard 8-track player squeaked to life, playing four hits all at once.

"Marge, I'm stuck."

"Oh, Ernest, I know. It's your car; you don't have to sell it if you're unsure. We can take the sign off and put it back under the carport."

"No, I'm stuck. The steering wheel is too tight. I need help getting out."

After a knee scraping head banging backbreaking extrication, Marge drove the El Camino to where Ernest busied himself untangling the hose and finding buckets and sponges.

Heaving herself heavily but unassisted from the vehicle Marge took charge of the washing.

"Ernest, you just sit and recover. Look, you scraped your forehead getting out of that thing. Just get me a chamois is all, a real one, you can't wash a car without a chamois cloth. Then you just sit and let me show you how it's done."

Ernest did as Marge instructed. After producing the chamois cloth he sat in his camp chair and watched her work. He noticed that she didn't miss a spot, noticed that her foremost parts were darkened damp from leaning to reach all of the roof and hood. He was in awe at the care and respect she showed the El Camino, ever mindful of scratches and streaks, and was suddenly surprised with wondering if she would be this way with children; their children.

When Marge playfully accused Ernest of checking her out and having a one-track mind, Ernest didn't deny it, only now he marveled at where this track could lead.

SOLD

Ernest's old El Camino had never shone so brightly as when Marge washed and waxed it, but he was ready to put it out by the road for sale. The car didn't fit him anymore, and besides maybe he needed to spend his time and money on other things.

He and Marge had no sooner placed the 'for sale' sign in the windshield when a big pickup piloted by a big-haired wiry little woman ripped to a stop in the gravel yard in front of the shop. The driver's side door swung open and Ilene Higginbottom swung out with it, dropping precariously from the height of her pickup truck, talking at Marge and extending a hand even before landing right in front of her on mismatched feet.

"Ilene."

"Yes, I see that," replied Marge, shaking her hand. "What can we do for you?"

"You have something I want."

"You'll have to be more specific."

"That El Camino; I need a truck that fits like a car. I am having too much trouble climbing in and out of this tank of a truck since my separation."

"Your separation?" Ernest puzzled how Ilene Higginbottom's status, single or otherwise, impacted vehicle entry, no matter the size of the truck.

"Yeah, since being separated from my leg, I have trouble stepping up." Both Ilene and Marge guffawed loudly while Ernest blushed and stammered out the possibility of a trade.

They came to terms, then sealed the deal over a beer. The women sat in the camp chairs while Ernest roosted on a stack of used tires, unable to keep up with Ilene's rapid fire prattle, and thinking his own thoughts anyway.

Ernest was thinking that he was glad to trade an El Camino that no longer fit for a truck that was roomy, sturdy, and practical. He marveled at how everything in his life was turning out just right. If only Ilene would go home soon, but she and Marge seemed to be having a good time. Ernest smiled and caught Marge's eye as one of the young robins took advantage of the puddle that remained from the car washing. Ilene, amazingly, paused in her talking to watch it too. And she looked at the two of them, Ernest and Marge, exchanging glances and remarking on the bird like proud parents. Then Ilene Higginbottom looked right at Ernest, long enough to make him turn colors, finally stating, "Ernest, you have a good thing here. You and Marge seem to be a good fit."

Ilene Higginbottom stood and thanked them both for the beer. "I'll be off. I got what I wanted."

They walked her to the El Camino.

WISHES

Once upon a time there lived an old man and an old woman. They had little in the way of possessions and wanted for nothing. Nothing unusual ever happened but every day they noticed small miracles as they gardened and gathered and occasionally fished in the stream that coursed through the meadow.

One day something unusual did happen. A talking fish offered them three wishes if they'd let it go.

The couple smiled at one another, not wishing to trade one of their days for anything. This amazing trout ended up in the same pan that more ordinary trout had.

HARMONIES

He sits in his stuffed armchair.

"Dad, aren't you going to help?"

"No Hope, I'm not. Gonna set here and look to be reading my magazine."

"You could at least play for us. I played for you when you picked the berries."

"Nope. Gonna just enjoy the sound of other people workin'."

Staccato at first, simple instructions, answers to questions. Then mother and daughter find their rhythm, the tempo quickening. Yelps from handling hot sterilized jars followed quickly by laughter. They giggle at one another's clef of bangs, curled by the steam.

He smiles, content.

RESURRECTIONS

There are still mason jars filled with sweet pickles, dill beans; jars of raspberry jelly, blackberry jelly, apple-butter. The potato bin is down to the last board but there should be enough.

Spindly white sprouts feel about for spring. These are rubbed off. The potatoes need to feed us a little longer before the leftovers are planted back in the ground.

The ice isn't yet out in the lake though peepers sing in the beaver meadow. Soon there will be fiddleheads and wild onions, then cattail greens.

Soon enough there will be freshly dug potatoes.

RETURN

Under winter's marbled evening sky

begin walking

keep going though snow is falling

rapidly covering your tracks.

Know the cold that winter brings

know also the dark

walk into the night

feel the sting and smart of cold

on your face and hands

feel the ache of it creeping

in all your limbs.

Go further; go till you no longer

feel even the dull ache.

Walk that far.

Then, shrouded with snow, stumbling in the dark

flailing and sinking through drifts

find your way back.

Return.

Only now can you know what it is you want

from the warm glow of light in a window.

ACKNOWLEDGEMENTS

In the Beginning were parents, both readers and storytellers still.

In the Formative formal education years were formal Teachers who encouraged me to write. Some still do. (Thank you Norma.)

In the Present are the friends who beta read and more for me. The encouragement, editing, and support of Carol, Jeannie, Janet, Francie, and Bonnie bettered this book. For their help and patience I am grateful. Writer and educator Norah Colvin bettered the writing and also the writer. To her and all the Rough Writers, ranch hands, buckaroos, leaders, and readers of Carrot Ranch Literary Community I extend a heartfelt thank you as vast as the western sky. Carrot Ranch is special. It's there that I found another Teacher, word warrior Charli Mills, who from her Ranch champions literary art worldwide. The story is that Perfessor Mills, an avid geologist, picked up a rock one day and found hiding underneath it a latent writer. Perfessor Mills also found a friend, one who appreciates all that she does for so many and who is grateful for all that she has done for me. 99 words aren't enough. Here are just two: *thank you*.

In the Future I'll write on, go where the prompts lead.

Always is my husband.

It's all Good.

THE AUTHOR

Born and raised in rural New England, D. Avery is never quite out of the woods, though she has been in other fields, including commercial floriculture, landscape gardening, and education.

D. Avery's poems and flash fiction can be found at *shiftnshake.wordpress.com*. She is a Rough Writer at Carrot Ranch Literary Community (*carrotranch.com*). D. Avery is the author of two books of poetry, **Chicken Shift** and **For the Girls**.